Charlestown bridge

Copp's Hill

Settlement house

Innie's tenement

Salem Street

Old North Church

Saint Leonard's

Nonna's kitchen

Innie's World
Boston in 1908

N

Settlement house library

UNDER COPP'S HILL

❧

by
Katherine Ayres

Published by Pleasant Company Publications
Text copyright © 2000 by Katherine Ayres
Illustrations copyright © 2000 by Pleasant Company
For information, address: Book Editor, Pleasant Company Publications,
8400 Fairway Place, P.O. Box 620998, Middleton, WI 53562.

Printed in the United States of America.
00 01 02 03 04 05 RRD 10 9 8 7 6 5 4 3 2 1

History Mysteries® and American Girl®
are trademarks of Pleasant Company.

PERMISSIONS & PICTURE CREDITS
The following individuals and organizations have generously given permission to reprint
illustrations contained in "A Peek into the Past": p. 155—cover of Paul Revere Pottery brochure
(colorized), artwork by Edith Brown, photo courtesy Marilee Boyd Meyer, Cambridge, MA;
pp. 156-157—Chelsea fire photo, courtesy of the Boston Public Library, Print Department;
photo of girl, Lewis W. Hine Collection, Milstein Division of U.S. History, Local History and
Genealogy, The New York Public Library, Astor, Lenox and Tilden Foundations (detail); passports,
photography by Karen Yamauchi for Chermayeff & Geismar Inc./MetaForm Inc.; Jane Addams
Collection, Swarthmore College Peace Collection; photo of Hull Street, courtesy of The Bostonian
Society (detail); pp. 158-159—folk dancing photo, courtesy of the Boston Public Library, Print
Department; club meeting photo, Old Dartmouth Historical Society—New Bedford Whaling
Museum; book, courtesy of the Department of Special Collections, General Library System,
University of Wisconsin-Madison; vase, collection of R.A. Ellison, photo courtesy Marilee Boyd
Meyer; plate, collection of Marilee Boyd Meyer; *Room in a Tenement Flat,* 1910, Jessie Tarbox
Beals, The Jacob A. Riis Collection, #502, Museum of the City of New York (detail); pp. 160-161—
Italian family, © Bettmann/Corbis; ransacked house, from the Archives of the YIVO Institute
for Jewish Research, New York, NY; Cossack soldier, Library of Congress (detail); North End
restaurant signs, Susan Cole Kelly, Boston, MA (detail); photo of girl, Salisbury Studios.

Cover and Map Illustrations: Troy Howell
Line Art: Laszlo Kubinyi
Editorial Direction: Peg Ross
Art Direction: Lynne Wells
Design: Laura Moberly and Justin Packard

Library of Congress Cataloging-in-Publication Data
Ayres, Katherine.
Under Copp's Hill / by Katherine Ayres.—1st ed.
p. cm. — (History mysteries ; 8)
"American girl."
Summary: In 1908, eleven-year-old Innie joins the library club at a settlement house that
serves immigrant families of Boston's North End, but when items and money disappear from
the settlement house, Innie's past as a troublemaker puts her under suspicion.

ISBN 1-58485-088-4 (pbk.) — ISBN 1-58485-089-2 (hc)
[1. Immigrants—Fiction. 2. Social settlements—Fiction. 3. Italian-Americans—Fiction.
4. Orphans—Fiction. 5. Boston (Mass.)—Fiction. 6. Mystery and detective stories.]
I. Title. II. Series.
PZ7.A9856 Un 2000 [Fic]—dc21   00-027883

To Steve and Lisa and Matthew

TABLE OF CONTENTS

CHAPTER I
CHELSEA'S BURNING

Innocenza Moretti crossed herself, slipped her rosary beads into her pocket, and turned down the aisle toward the door of Saint Leonard's Church. Behind her she could hear the slow tread of her grandmother's feet, but she couldn't bear to wait for Nonna even though she knew she ought to. Mass seemed to have gone on for a long time this morning, and sitting still made Innie itch.

As Innie made her way through the crowd of old ladies in long black dresses and shawls, she felt a tug on her elbow. Her cousin Teresa had caught up to her, and together they stepped outside into a bright April noon.

"Mama's making meatballs," Teresa said. "I can't wait."

"Me neither," Innie said. Zia Rachela was the best cook in the North End. Weekdays, Innie and Nonna had to fix suppers for the seven *bordanti*—young men, all fresh off the boat from Italy, who lodged with them in their downstairs flat. But on Sundays the men ate sausages, cheese, and bread by themselves so Innie and Nonna could eat upstairs with Teresa's family. Innie loved those Sunday dinners in her cousin's flat, surrounded by the joking and loud laughter of Zia Rachela's big family.

Innie took a deep breath of the salty spring breeze that blew up from Boston Harbor. Then she stopped and sniffed carefully. "Teresa, do you smell something? Smoke, maybe?"

Teresa turned to her with that worried look that always made Innie want to scream. "Maybe it's just the incense from church."

"No, it's not. Incense smells sweet." Innie scanned the sky. To the north, across the harbor, she saw a smudge of gray. "There! See the smoke?" she said, pointing. "Let's find out where it's coming from."

"Fine, but we can't let Nonna see the smoke," Teresa whispered.

Innie glanced back at the church and saw Nonna walk slowly down the steps, with Zia Rachela holding one elbow and Teresa's older sister, Carmela, holding the other. Carmela wore her trim blue American suit with a wide-brimmed hat. To Innie, she looked like a spring flower among the old-fashioned black dresses that the older women wore.

Teresa took three steps sideways as the women neared, putting herself between Nonna and the patch of smoky sky. "Mama?" she asked. "May Innie and I walk along the water for a little while? Please? It's such a pretty day."

"A walk?" Nonna scowled. "And who helps get dinner on the table, huh?"

Zia Rachela smiled. "Fifteen minutes, girls. Then come right home and get busy. Just don't get your dresses dirty."

"*Mannaggia l'America!* These girls don't behave right." Nonna pointed a bony finger at Innie. "Don't be late, you."

"*Grazie,* Mama. *Grazie,* Nonna." Teresa stood planted until Nonna had turned away from the smoke.

Innie tapped her foot on the sidewalk. Teresa was good at asking for favors, but it took her so long. "Hurry!" Innie whispered. "I want to see what's making that smoke."

The cousins left the church behind and headed north toward the water. At every street corner, clumps of men stood talking. Women bustled past, hurrying home to their kitchens. "Let's go to the burying ground," Innie said, after she'd nearly bumped into a man. "It won't be so crowded there, and we can see a long way from the top of Copp's Hill."

"I don't know why you have to look at every puff of smoke," Teresa said. "You, of all people. I'd think you'd try *not* to look."

At the top of Salem Street, they turned onto Hull Street and passed the Old North Church, where a long time ago, American patriots had hung warning lanterns in the tall steeple for Paul Revere to see. Just past the church, the girls entered the gates of the stone-walled burying ground. In spite of the crooked old tombstones, Innie liked to walk here, where trees and grass grew all around. Standing on Copp's Hill, a person could breathe fresh, salty sea air, for the harbor lay less than a block away, at the bottom of the hill.

Innie pulled on Teresa's hand, tugging her along the brick pathway, past trees just starting to show green tips, to the top of the hill. Below them, water gleamed blue. The harbor stretched out to Charlestown, then bent north. The smoke showed clearly now, a dark plume rising from East Boston or beyond.

"See, I told you. It *is* a fire." No sooner had Innie spoken than a loud boom echoed across the water. As she stood watching, yellow and orange flames shot into the sky. Innie bit down hard on her bottom lip.

"Looks like a bad fire," Teresa said. "I hope Mama got Nonna home before she heard that noise."

Another boom sounded, and a third, setting off more flares. Innie caught her breath and fingered the rosary beads in her pocket.

Teresa squeezed Innie's other hand. "You all right?"

"I'm *fine*. It's Nonna who gets upset, not me."

"But, Innie . . ."

Innie yanked her hand away. She wished Teresa would mind her own business. "How many times do I have to tell you? Nonna remembers, not me. It's been nearly ten years—I was just two. I don't remember anything."

Teresa tried to catch her hand again, but Innie resisted. She turned and faced her cousin.

"I really don't remember," she repeated. "Not the fire, not the smoke." She sighed and looked out over the water where the gray plumes thickened and twisted together, darkening a wider patch of sky. "Look, I was a baby. I don't even remember Mama and Papà. Not one thing. So there." She tried to shake off the gloominess. "What do you think, Teresa? What exploded?"

"I don't know, Innie. Come on, let's go home. We gotta help Mama."

Innie studied the sky for another moment. The cloud of smoke grew thicker and wider every time she blinked. Some fire, that was. It would eat up a lot of buildings, and people too, unless they could run away fast. Her lips began a silent prayer. She let Teresa tug her down the hill and out the gates to Hull Street, where they turned left and made their way toward the bustle of Salem Street and home.

⚬❧

As she climbed the dark, narrow staircase of the tenement with Teresa, Innie could smell meatballs cooking. When they reached the crowded kitchen of the second-floor flat, Innie's stomach growled, begging to be fed. Zia Rachela, wrapped in a white apron, bustled at the big black stove, while Teresa's brother Antonio tried to snitch bits of pasta from a bubbling pot.

Innie breathed in the spicy smell, then checked the table and counted plates. Carmela had already set the table, Innie's usual job.

"Late again. You been bad, Innocenza," Antonio said. "Maybe you don't get to eat today." He laughed.

"Hush, you. Stop bothering our Innie." Zia Rachela smacked Antonio's fingers, but that didn't stop him from snitching. He was thirteen and a pest.

Zia Rachela ladled pasta into bowls, and Innie and her two girl cousins carried the bowls to the table and set out sauce and grated cheese. The family gathered around. Innie's uncle, Zio Giovanni, sat at one end of the table, with the three boys along one side in order of age— Benito, the hard worker, next to his papa, then Mario, who smiled so nice, and Antonio last. On the other side of the table, Innie squeezed between Teresa and Carmela. Zia Rachela set down a big platter of meatballs and took her place next to Nonna, closest to the stove.

Sitting between her beautiful cousins, Innie felt bony, but it wasn't for lack of eating. Zia Rachela always said Innie was too full of mischief to sit still, so she burned up all her meals before they could settle anywhere.

Still, Innie wished she looked more like Teresa. They both had the same long dark hair, dark eyes, and clear olive skin. But Teresa's face was smooth and soft instead of skinny. Teresa would grow up to be just as pretty as Zia Rachela and Carmela, Innie thought, while *she* would probably always look like a crow.

Her thoughts were interrupted by Antonio's voice. "There's a big fire over in Chelsea. You should have heard the noise. Me and my pals were right by the water when it started," he bragged.

"Instead of in church, where you belong," Zia Rachela scolded.

"Now, Mama." Mario sent a big smile down the table. "You and Nonna do enough praying for the whole family."

"Somebody needs to say a lot of prayers. Chelsea's burning," Zia Rachela said. She crossed herself.

Without meaning to, Innie did the same.

Nonna sat up straight and glared at Antonio. "Fire? Where's a fire? Chelsea, you say?" She shoved back her chair and stood, making the sign of the cross, then hurried from the room without another word. The kitchen door banged behind her.

Carmela glared at Antonio. "Big-mouth. Should I go help her, Mama?"

Zia Rachela shook her head. "Stay and eat. There's no help for Nonna when there's a fire, except for her prayers."

Innie sighed, wishing she could do something to make her grandmother feel better. If she closed her eyes, Innie could picture exactly what Nonna would do—go into her little room at the back of the flat and kneel on the bare floor, elbows resting on her bed. Then her fingers would begin counting the beads of her rosary as she murmured the familiar prayers. But at least the fire was in Chelsea, Innie thought. So far away that it wouldn't touch her own family. Except for Nonna, of course. Every fire touched Nonna.

"Stop with the fire talk," Zio Giovanni said. "This family knows plenty about fires and praying. Talk about something else. Something happy."

Everybody went silent, as if his words had frozen their tongues. Then Carmela cleared her throat. "I . . . I have some news, Papà."

"Well, then. Tell your news."

"I was going to talk to you private, Papà. But you want something happy? I got a new job. I don't have to go back to the shirt factory. A pottery is opening over on Hull Street. It runs full-time, and they want me for a decorator."

Innie turned to stare at Carmela.

"What? Pottery decorator? What kind of job is that for a girl?" Zio Giovanni asked.

"It's a good job, Papà. I'll be painting nice pictures on plates and bowls. Miss Brown, the lady who runs the pottery, says I have a steady hand."

"The job pays good?" Zio Giovanni tapped his spoon against his bowl.

"Seven dollars a week, and I can walk there, so I don't have to pay streetcars." Carmela smiled and turned to her mother. "It's nice work too, Mama. No hot, noisy machines, no poking my fingers with needles, no Mr. Johnson snooping over my shoulder to make sure my seams go straight."

"You got a lady boss, that Miss Brown?" Zio Giovanni said. "Sounds good. I don't like the way those factory men treat girls."

"So it's all right, Papà?"

He nodded at Carmela.

"This is good news," Zia Rachela said. "I like you working nearby."

Next to her, Innie could feel Carmela shift in her chair.

"*Grazie,* Papà, Mama. I'll start this week then. But there's more. I want Teresa and Innie to come too. The pottery is part of a new settlement house for girls in the North End. They give classes one day a week for younger girls—sewing and knitting."

Sewing! Innie shot her cousin a look. She opened her mouth to protest but felt Carmela give her a stiff pinch on the leg.

"It's a good place to learn things. American things," Carmela continued, looking at her papa. "Then when the girls get old enough, they can work at the pottery too. Earn good money. With a nice woman boss."

Zia Rachela frowned. "But the girls have school. And chores."

"Younger girls, they go after school," Carmela told her. "It's just one afternoon a week, so they can still help you and Nonna. And the classes might even help them with school."

"Oh yeah, Teresa and Innie need all the help they can get." Antonio smirked across the table. Innie stuck out her tongue at him.

Her uncle spoke again. "They won't be out after dark?"

"No. Four until six. Home in time for supper. Please."

"All right, then. As long as they get their chores done." With that, Zio Giovanni helped himself to salad, then passed the plate. Benito, Mario, and Antonio nearly emptied the plate before it reached the girls. But for once, Innie didn't mind. The sooner the meal was done, the sooner she could tell Carmela just what she thought of her meddling.

After dinner, Zio Giovanni left to stroll the neighborhood. The boys ran down the stairs and onto the street in search of their pals. Zia Rachela went to check on Nonna. Innie, Teresa, and Carmela started to clean up the kitchen. Teresa poured hot water into the dishpan from a kettle on the stove.

Innie added soap, shoved a load of sticky spoons into the hot water, and began scrubbing. "You think you can boss everybody in the world, Carmela? You may be twenty-one and grown-up, but you're not my sister. You can't make me go to some settlement house and sew."

"That's how much you know, Innie." Carmela stood with her hands on her hips. "I'm doing you a favor is what. This isn't just about sewing."

"What is it about, then?" Teresa asked.

"It's a library club for girls. We sew a little, but mostly we read books, sing songs, and listen to the Victrola. We can even borrow books and take them home."

Books! The word boomed in Innie's ears just as the fire had earlier. In school she had to share her books with two or three girls. And for a fast reader like Innie, that meant waiting to turn each page until the other girls were ready. *Getting to borrow a book and read it all by yourself,* Innie thought, *that would be like having Sunday dinner every day of the week.* "How come I don't know about this?" Innie frowned.

"Like I said, the settlement house is new. Besides, you think I'd tell the boys or Papà about a club for reading books? He went to school two years, maybe three, back in Italy. He already thinks we study too long in America."

"So how does this club work, Carmela?" Teresa asked.

Carmela explained and Innie listened hard, trying to remember everything. One afternoon or evening each week, a group of girls the same age would meet, read books, and talk about them. They'd learn songs and folk dances. Girls in sixth grade, like Innie and Teresa, would meet on Wednesday afternoons.

Then Carmela got a bossy look on her face again and began a long list of do's and don'ts aimed right at Innie.

Innie imitated her exactly.

"Look, you," Carmela scolded. "The settlement house is a good place. I already promised you would come."

Innie scowled. "I don't like people promising for me without asking," she said. There'd been too much of that in her life already. "But I'll go this time. On Wednesday. For the books."

"You'll go Monday and Tuesday, too, this week, to help unpack books. They're still moving in. I'll talk to Mama and get you out of your chores."

"Who says?" Innie argued.

"I do," Carmela said. "Look, Innie. If you behave yourself and don't make trouble for once in your life, you could have a real good time. That's why I said you'd help—so the ladies will think you're nice. And you *will* be nice, because I work there, and if you act up I could lose my new job."

Innie could feel her temper begin to simmer. She opened her mouth to tell Carmela just what she thought, but Teresa interrupted.

"Wait, who are the ladies?"

"Miss Guerrier, who runs the library clubs, and Miss Brown, who runs the pottery. They live on the top floor in the new house. They're wonderful."

We'll see about that, Innie thought. But at least there were books. Books were always wonderful.

That evening, Innie and Teresa climbed past old lady Napoli's flat on the third floor of the tenement, all the way up to the roof. Looking out over the jumbled rooftops and narrow, crooked streets, they saw people all over the North End standing outside, watching the sky, and talking excitedly. Even three stories up, Innie could hear the hum of raised voices. She could smell the fire.

Smoke hung like a heavy curtain over the whole of Boston. It burned Innie's eyes. To the north, the sky glowed a deep orange-red. That fire in Chelsea was bad and getting worse. Innie wondered when the firefighters would be able to douse it. "Soon," she whispered softly. "Put the fire out soon."

"You'll be all right?" Teresa asked.

"Sure, sure," Innie said.

Later that night, though, Innie couldn't sleep. Nonna was still praying, keeping her vigil in the small room they shared behind the kitchen. Innie huddled under the blanket on her cot, staring into the darkness. She kept remembering that orange sky and wondering. *How many people will burn this time? How many mothers and fathers? How many girls will become orphans tonight?*

Chapter 2
A Secret Ride

By Monday the fire had stopped burning, but smoke still shrouded Boston. On the way to school, in class, at recess, everyone talked about the Chelsea fire. Newsboys shouted and teachers spoke in grim, careful tones until Innie wanted to plug her ears.

Everywhere she turned, Innie heard rumors. Ten thousand homes and businesses had burned. No, twenty thousand. The mayor had called up the police to keep order. No, he'd called up the army and the navy and the marines. He'd closed off Chelsea so no robbers could get in. No, he'd made everyone in Chelsea leave.

By the end of the school day, she couldn't wait to escape the hubbub by going to the settlement house. She and Teresa climbed Salem Street's steep hill, where pockets of people gathered in front of shops to gossip in loud Italian. At Hull Street, they turned and walked the half block to number eighteen, a large, redbrick row house right across from the burying ground. *This house is too grand to be a tenement. It must have belonged to a rich person,* Innie thought. Its windows were tall and shining, the front door freshly painted, the front steps scrubbed clean. The door was propped open. Innie and Teresa peered inside.

A slender young woman came toward them, smiling. "Are you here to help? Let me guess, Carmela's sister and cousin? She said you'd come." She stuck out a dirty hand, looked at it, wiped it on her apron, and stuck it out again. "I'm Miss Guerrier. Welcome. We can surely use your help today." The woman had gray eyes and dark hair done up in a loose knot. She spoke in a crisp, clipped Yankee voice, but Innie thought she seemed friendly.

They all shook hands, and then the girls followed Miss Guerrier up a flight of stairs to the second floor. She led them through a wide hallway into a large room with tall windows along one wall. The other walls were lined with bookshelves. Afternoon sun peeked through the windows and made patterns on the dark wood floor. In one corner, another girl knelt with pails and rags, scrubbing a shelf. The room smelled so clean it stung Innie's nose.

"That fire made quite a mess," the lady began. "As you can see, we're scrubbing the meeting room today. The walls are done, but the shelves need work. Tomorrow we'll bring books and unpack. Matela, these girls have offered to help, as you have. They're cousins, Innie and Teresa Moretti. I'll be upstairs working on the third floor. I'll be down in a while to see how you're doing." Miss Guerrier smiled and hurried back into the hallway.

Innie pushed up the sleeves of her dress. It wasn't hard to see which shelves needed cleaning, but Innie thought it might be polite to ask the other girl where to begin. After all, she'd gotten here first. "Want some help?"

"Yes, please." The girl turned to them and smiled. "Plenty dirt for three. I'm Matela Rosen."

Innie smiled back at the girl. Matela was small and thin, with dark hair and pale skin.

"Are you in one of the library clubs?" Teresa asked.

"Not yet," Matela said. "But soon. Wednesday."

"We're new, too. And we'll be Wednesday afternoon girls like you." Innie bent and picked up a rag. "All right if I wash the next bookshelf?"

"Sure. Miss Guerrier, she says start at the top, scrub down. Change the water when it gets dirty. There is a tap in the kitchen. Lucky for us the walls are done. That smoke, it goes everywhere."

Smoke again, Innie thought. Was there no place in Boston she could hide from news of the burning? "I'm tired of hearing about that fire."

Teresa pulled a pail close to some dirty shelves. "I'm sure Mama's busy at home too, scrubbing soot off our walls."

Nonna was too, Innie decided. Now that the fire was over, Nonna would scrub until her hands grew raw, making all the signs of fire disappear.

"I, too, am tired of fire," Matela said. "In the old country . . ."

Innie looked at her sharply. "What happened in the old country?" she asked.

Matela shrugged. "They burn things back in Russia."

Surely Matela didn't mean that the way it sounded, Innie thought. "What . . . what do you mean?" she asked.

"The czar's soldiers. First they burn the *shul* where Papa prays. Then some barns. Papa says houses burn next, so we go to America. Two years now, almost three, we live here."

Soldiers burning innocent people's barns and houses? The very idea made Innie's stomach hurt.

"How come we don't know you, then?" Teresa asked. "Do you go to Hancock School?"

Matela slopped her rag into the pail with a splash. "Yes. Hancock. But I . . . When we come, they put me with babies in grade one. I am nine then and big. But a greenhorn—so new—I have no English."

Teresa nodded. "We had big girls in our class too. Innie and I, we're in sixth grade. I'm twelve, and Innie turns twelve this summer." She stood and hauled her pail of dirty water out into the hallway.

"I am twelve in summer also. And I am still a little green," Matela explained to Innie. "But I don't let them keep me with babies. I learn quick and I jump. I'm hurrying to finish grade five. This summer, I study hard and learn grade six. In the year to come, I go to seven."

"With us," Innie finished. "But that's lots of studying."

"I don't mind," Matela said shyly. "I love books. And Papa says if America gives you school for free, you must take with both hands."

"I'd like your papa," Innie said. She scrubbed hard with her rag and smiled, trying to imagine a family that thought reading books was a good idea, especially for daughters. That was nicer than thinking about fires.

The three girls finished the shelves and then wiped down the windowsills until they shone. "Let's do the floor too," Innie suggested. "It's all spotty from our pails. I'll get clean water."

Innie lugged two pails down the hallway to the back of the house. When she stepped into the kitchen, she could hardly believe such a room existed—large, bright, and so clean, with a big white sink that gleamed. Just these two rooms, the meeting room and the kitchen, were larger than the flat she lived in with Nonna and seven lodgers. And here, they had running water right in the kitchen—you didn't have to lug it from the hallway.

While the first pail filled, Innie cracked open a door to one of the cabinets and peeked inside. Shiny pots and pans of different sizes filled the shelves. They looked brand-new. She opened another door and saw colorful pottery mugs lined up like soldiers in rows. She heard a sound that might have been footsteps and quickly closed the door, then lifted the pail of fresh water out of the sink.

When the second pail was full, she lugged both back to the meeting room, water slopping out onto her skirt.

"Innie, you're soaked," Teresa said. "Nonna will scold."

Innie shrugged. "So Nonna will scold. *La vita è così.*"

"Pardon? What does that mean?" Matela frowned. "*La vita . . .*"

"*La vita è così?* That's Italian," Innie said. "Nonna, our grandmother, she's always saying it. It means 'Life is like that,' or something."

Matela nodded. "*Azoy gayt es,* 'so it goes.' That's Yiddish. My grandfather back in Russia, he says these words. At least I hope so. I miss him. I hope he's still all right."

Innie set down the sloshing pails and knelt to scrub, peering sideways at Matela, studying her. *So,* she thought. *This girl's got holes in her life too.*

With three girls working, it didn't take long to scrub the floor. Afterward, while Matela and Teresa hauled the pails of dirty water to the kitchen, Innie decided to explore.

Between the meeting room and kitchen, she found a dining room with a shiny wood table, and chairs set neatly around. At one end, near a window, stood a piano. Back in the wide hallway, Innie noticed a row of coat hooks along one side, and on the other, the stairway she and Teresa had taken earlier. It was a grand, fancy stairway with a smooth, polished banister. Innie walked closer and let her fingers glide over the dark wood of that banister. It felt so slick, even a spider would fall off, she thought. So slick, it would be fun to slide down.

Did she dare? She looked around. Nobody was in sight, and so what if Teresa or Matela came out of the kitchen and saw her? She climbed the stairs to the third floor quickly, on tiptoe. When she reached the landing, she hopped up on the railing, caught her balance, and shoved off.

Whoosh! What a ride!

At the bottom, she jumped down and grinned. Did she have time for another ride? she wondered. Sure, why not? She'd almost reached the third floor when Miss Guerrier suddenly appeared at the landing.

"Innie? Whatever are you doing here?"

"Um, I just came to tell you that we finished scrubbing the bookshelves, Miss. And the floor too."

"I see. Thank you very much then. But, Innie, club girls don't come up these stairs unless invited."

"Yes, Miss. Sorry, Miss." *All right,* Innie thought, *so I can't ride the banister again. Worse things could happen.* At least she'd gotten to ride once.

CHAPTER 3
MOVING DAY

On Tuesday, the hubbub about the fire continued. On the way to school, Innie closed her eyes to the horrible newspaper pictures showing piles of blackened stones where houses used to be. She crossed the street to avoid groups of men gossiping on the street corners.

Still, the news seeped into her mind. Churches were asking for donations of food and clothing for people whose homes had burned. Soldiers patrolled Chelsea, searching for bodies. And the mayor really *had* closed off Chelsea from the rest of Boston. Innie tried to push the terrible fire out of her mind and concentrate on getting through the school day so she could return to the settlement house.

That afternoon the weather turned gray, and the walk up Salem Street chilled Innie all the way through. Teresa and Matela were shivering too. On both sides of the street, shops and tenements loomed, casting long, cold shadows on the sidewalk. People hurried past, clutching coats and shawls tightly against the damp. Even the horses pulling wagons and hacks through the narrow streets looked cold to Innie.

As she, Teresa, and Matela reached Hull Street, they passed a cluster of older girls unloading heavy crates from a horse-drawn cart on the street.

Miss Guerrier stood at the door to the settlement house. When she saw the three girls, she smiled. "You did a wonderful job cleaning the shelves yesterday," she said. "We're moving books. Would you like to help unpack?"

"Sure," Innie said. Teresa and Matela nodded.

Miss Guerrier led the way upstairs and through a maze of crates into the meeting room. Today, a thick woven rug with bright patterns in red and gold lay over the clean floor. Simple curtains framed all the windows. That Miss Guerrier had sure been busy.

"The books are packed in alphabetical order, by author," she explained. "Let's start here with the *A*'s and move around the room. And be sure to leave extra space on each shelf. We'll be buying more books soon."

Books and more books. Innie thought of the million places she could visit in all those books. She felt like a starving child might feel visiting the market stalls and seeing boxes and bins overflowing with food. And, as if the crates of books already here weren't enough, these Yankee ladies would buy more! Innie itched to touch a new, perfect book. At school the books were all smudged, and she'd never read one that still had all its pages.

She located a crate marked *A* and opened the flaps. With careful fingers, she drew out a thick green book and traced the title—*Little Women,* by Louisa May Alcott. Inside she saw a drawing of four smiling girls and their mother. *I must read that,* Innie decided, and set it on the shelf. As she unpacked, she discovered eight more books by Miss Alcott. They'd keep her reading for a long time.

In the two hours between school and suppertime, Innie, Teresa, and Matela emptied crate after crate of books. When the last crate was empty and her skirt was covered with dust and grime, Innie returned to the *A* shelf and studied the row of books by Miss Alcott. Quickly, she hid *Little Women* at the back of the shelf, behind the other books. At the club meeting tomorrow, Carmela had explained, each girl would be allowed to borrow a book for a whole week. Innie didn't want anyone else to get *Little Women* first. She was shoving books together to hide it when Teresa crept up next to her.

"What are you doing, Innie?"

"Shhh. I'm just hiding a book that I want to borrow tomorrow."

"Well, stop it. Messing with the books like that, it looks like you're stealing one."

"Stealing one what?" Matela asked, as she joined them.

"Nothing. I'm just hiding a book," Innie said.

"You'll get in trouble," Teresa warned, shaking her head just as Nonna would.

"*La vita è così*," Innie replied.

"Here, hide it better." Matela quickly helped arrange the *A* shelf.

"Thanks. Let's go now." Innie stepped toward the door, but she stopped when she heard loud voices coming from the hall. She turned toward Teresa and Matela and put a finger to her lips. "Shhh."

". . . yes, I'm sure. A crate is missing. When I went to make us a pot of tea, I couldn't find the teapot, or the tea."

Innie didn't recognize the voice, but she could tell that the woman who spoke was upset.

"My dear Miss Brown, don't worry so. Surely on moving day, one might misplace a crate. Did you look in the kitchen?"

That sounded like Miss Guerrier's calm voice. Innie inched closer to the open doorway.

"I've scoured our entire apartment upstairs and searched the kitchen here as well—with no luck, I'm sorry to say. The crate is just gone. The thought of someone, an intruder, being in our home . . ."

"Please, Miss Brown. Let's think about this. We've had delivery men coming and going for some time. Perhaps one of them simply moved it."

Innie liked the way Miss Guerrier was speaking. She sounded confident and strong.

"Now what was in the crate, dear? Do you recall?"

"Of course I recall. I packed a variety of things we could eat during the move—tins of saltines, bags of walnuts and raisins, two tins of our Earl Grey tea. And as there was still room in the crate, I tucked your silver teapot in, wrapped with towels to protect it."

"My grandmother's teapot? I see." Miss Guerrier's voice had gone quiet.

Innie caught her breath. She'd never even seen a silver teapot, but it sounded important. Plus, it wasn't just Miss Guerrier's—it was her grandmother's.

Innie heard footsteps and motioned to Teresa and Matela, but before they could move from the doorway, both ladies walked in.

"You girls. You've been here working for some time?" The woman who spoke was shorter and plumper than Miss Guerrier and looked mussed from moving. She must be Carmela's Miss Brown.

"Y–yes, Miss. Unpacking books." Innie stammered.

"Have you seen anyone who appeared suspicious?" Miss Guerrier asked in a softer voice.

"No, Miss," Matela said.

"Thank you, then. You may go." Miss Guerrier tried to smile, but Innie could tell the lady didn't feel like smiling, and Innie didn't much blame her.

As the girls stepped down into the hall, Innie heard Miss Brown say quietly, "You know, I'm sure that I saw one of them in the kitchen yesterday, nosing around."

Innie swallowed hard. She *had* been snooping, but just for a minute.

"Let's search the apartment again, shall we?" said Miss Guerrier. "I'm sure it's just a mix-up."

"I hope it's just a mix-up," Innie whispered as she stepped outdoors with Teresa and Matela. She didn't want any trouble to upset a nice lady like Miss Guerrier.

"They'll find it soon. It would be easy to lose one crate in such a big house," Teresa said. "Come on, Innie, let's go home. Will you walk with us, Matela? You walk down Salem Street, don't you?"

"Yes. I will like that."

"I'll like it too," Innie declared, flinging one arm around Teresa's shoulder and one around Matela's. "And we'll be Wednesday afternoon girls together, starting tomorrow."

❧

As they turned the corner at Old North Church, Innie caught sight of her cousin Antonio and one of his pals. Once Innie and Teresa reached their tenement and said good-bye to Matela, Antonio stomped across the street and stopped them. "Who's that girl? She don't look Italian."

"So what?" Innie said.

"So Papà might not like it. You stick to your own

kind or I'll tell." He stood right in front of them with his feet planted wide.

"Don't tell, Tony," Teresa said. "I'll save my dessert for you. Please?"

"I'll think about it." He poked a finger at Innie. "You, Innocenza, you stay away from that strange girl. Don't you get my sister in trouble again. *Capisci?*"

"Sure, sure." Innie shrugged and headed inside. In the kitchen, Nonna was stirring something in a big pot on the stove. She waved her spoon at Innie. "Ah, *bambina,* cold day outside. Come. Warm yourself by the stove."

As Innie stepped closer, Nonna took a look at her dress and began to scold. "Look, you. Yesterday wet, today dirty. With seven *bordanti* to feed, you think I got time to wash dresses every night? Why can't you behave good, like Teresa? Ah, maybe I should send you to the Sisters sooner."

Please, not that again. Innie shook her head. "I'm sorry, Nonna."

Nonna pointed with the spoon. "Go! Brush off the dirt. Then help lay the table. The *bordanti* come soon."

Innie slipped into the back room and piled her coat and schoolbooks on her cot. She shook the dirt off her skirt. Then she set bowls and spoons out on the table for the lodgers and lifted the lid of the heavy iron pot on the stove. Spaghetti with peas tonight. Good. And tomorrow, she and Teresa would become real Wednesday afternoon girls.

So who cared about a scolding, anyway? Or that greedy Antonio with his two desserts?

❧

Later, as darkness fell, Innie lay on her cot listening to the muffled creaks of the men in the front rooms settling in for the night. Nearby, she heard Nonna's bed shift again and again as the old woman rolled and tossed. That fire had sure upset Nonna, and until she finally fell asleep, Innie would hear every rustle.

She tucked her blanket around her shoulders and crept into the kitchen, where she pulled a chair close to the stove to stay warm.

Fires—they made Innie's stomach knot up sometimes, but other times it almost felt as if the flames spoke to her and called her by name. She stared at the stove, banked down for the night. Only thin lines of red showed.

She tugged open the door and looked into the fiery coals. "Oh Mama, oh Papà, where are you now? Why can't I ever remember what you look like?"

She got no answers, but she really didn't expect any. Just talking to Mama and Papà helped push away the chill, so she kept talking to them for a while. And in the dim light, she let her mind carry her away to a place where nobody ever got burned or hurt, and nobody ever felt lonely.

CHAPTER 4
NEW GIRLS

Welcome to the library club." Miss Guerrier sat in a low chair at one end of the meeting room, with the Wednesday afternoon girls sitting in a circle on the rug in front of her. The room was so grand, even twenty girls didn't make it feel crowded. Today Miss Guerrier looked grand too, with soft lace edging the collar and cuffs of her white blouse. Innie closed her eyes and imagined herself growing into such a fine woman and living in such a splendid house.

"We have three new members today, girls—Teresa and Innie Moretti, and Matela Rosen. Please make sure you welcome them to the club." Miss Guerrier pointed in Innie's direction.

Innie looked around the room and felt her face grow warm. Some of the girls she knew from school, including a couple she wished she didn't know—Maria and Stella.

Those two were always tattling to the teacher for little things, like when Innie teased them for being scared to turn cartwheels, or when she hid their homework in the wrong desk. Other girls were strangers, and they were looking at her. It made her wish, for once, that she played quiet games in the playground and kept her dress tidy.

Miss Guerrier went on. "We're also very excited to have moved into our new building here on Hull Street. Miss Brown and I think that deserves a celebration." She turned toward a doorway, and two older girls walked in carrying trays. The smell of chocolate filled the room.

After a long day in school and a cold, damp walk to the settlement house, the scent made Innie's mouth water. Soon every girl in the room was warming her hands around a sturdy mug of the hot chocolate. The older girls disappeared again and returned with plates of large, round sugar cookies. Innie took a bite and let the sweetness sit on her tongue, melting slowly.

Even if they didn't have books here, this club would be wonderful, Innie thought. It was warm and clean and pretty. Nice ladies fed you treats. People didn't scold you or boss you around. Instead, they said *please* and *thank you.* This was some place, all right. She'd come here forever.

"We'll start a new book today," Miss Guerrier said. "It's called *The Prince and the Pauper,* by Mark Twain. I'm sure you've all heard about princes, but does anyone know what a pauper is?"

Innie didn't. Nobody else raised a hand to answer.

"Well, then," Miss Guerrier said. "A prince is the son of a king, a rich man. A pauper is a very poor man—a person who lives in a desperate situation. This book is about one of each. Shall we begin? *In the ancient city of London, on a certain autumn day in the second quarter of the sixteenth century, a boy was born to a poor family of the name of Canty, who did not want him. . . .*"

Miss Guerrier read on for half an hour, telling the story of poor Tom Canty and how he met the Crown Prince of England. The prince wanted to sample the footraces and river play of rabble boys, so he traded places with poor Tom. Innie sat so still she hardly breathed, but her mind fairly flew along with the words. Oh, to be that Tom Canty, turned into a prince, or a princess in her case. She felt like royalty, all right, sitting in a cozy room sipping chocolate while a spring rain speckled the windows.

"More next week," Miss Guerrier said, closing the pages at last. "Now you may select a book to borrow for the week. Please sign your full name on the card in the pocket. Then leave the card at the desk before you go."

Oh, Innie thought, *how could you choose just one book when there were so many?*

As girls left the circle to browse, Innie hurried to the shelf where she'd hidden *Little Women* the day before. She reached to the back of the shelf to retrieve it, but it wasn't there. Frowning, she selected another book by Miss Alcott, then checked the nearby shelves and finally spotted *Little Women* sitting crookedly in plain sight on the D shelf. She tugged on Teresa's arm to show her just as Miss Brown entered the doorway carrying a crate. Innie saw Miss Guerrier look up in surprise and walk quickly across the room to join Miss Brown.

Most of the girls were already waiting in line across the room to check out their books. But Innie and Teresa stayed where they were, partly hidden by bookshelves, and listened as Miss Brown spoke quietly to Miss Guerrier.

"Look, I found the missing crate. But the food's gone."

How bad is that? Innie wondered. *It was just some nuts and raisins and crackers, wasn't it?*

Miss Guerrier lifted out a tea tin and smiled. "I guess the thief doesn't care for Earl Grey. He left both tins of tea for us."

"The ruffian may not like our tea, but he certainly coveted your teapot. It's gone, along with the food."

No, thought Innie. *Not her grandmother's silver teapot. Poor Miss Guerrier.*

"Gone. Oh, my." Miss Guerrier sighed. "And where did you discover this crate?"

"That's the oddest thing. It was down in the basement, tucked behind the kiln. If I hadn't been arranging the shelves, I might have missed it."

"And of course you searched for the teapot?"

"Everywhere. It's truly gone."

No, Innie thought. *It can't be gone.*

"Oh, Miss Brown."

"We'll have the locksmith come," Miss Brown said. "If there's a thief around, we need a lock on our apartment door. Wouldn't hurt to have the front door latches checked as well."

Good for you, Miss Brown, Innie decided. She looked away from the ladies and scanned the bookshelf once more. Maybe that thief had been in here too, searching through the books.

"Look at this, Teresa," she whispered. "Somebody moved my book."

Matela joined them. "What do you whisper about?" she asked. "It is secret? Or will you tell me?"

"Innie says someone moved a book, as if that's a crime."

"I didn't say it was a crime. But how could it happen? Look." Innie picked up *Little Women* and showed it to Matela. "Yesterday I hid this book. You even helped me, remember? But we were the last girls in this room yesterday and the first to get here today. So who moved it?"

"Stop looking for trouble," Teresa scolded.

"Hush, Teresa. Maybe the person who stole from the ladies was messing about in here. Did you hear them, Matela? Miss Brown found the missing crate, but things had been taken from it."

"Yes, I hear them talk," Matela said.

Teresa shook her head. "Innie, you're making a big

fuss over nothing. A silver teapot—that's important. But a moved book?"

"It's *not* nothing, Teresa," Innie argued. "There's been a thief in the house."

Matela smiled and raised her eyebrows. "Maybe not a thief. Things are moved, not stolen. When odd things happen in my house, Mama blames a *mazik*." She made her voice sound low and spooky. "So maybe a *mazik* comes here too—in the night."

"What's a *mazik*?" Teresa asked. Innie had never heard of such a thing, either.

"You don't know *maziks*?" Matela explained. "*Maziks* make mischief. They are naughty, wicked spirits. They come and go, but nobody sees. My *bubbe*—my grandmother—back in Russia, she tells me all about them."

Teresa glanced out the window at the burying ground just across the street, and her face went pale. "Do you mean a ghost?"

"Come on, Teresa, there are no such things as ghosts," Innie said. But a shiver ran down her back all the same.

"Look," she said. "I'm going to hide another book in the same spot." She pulled a blue-covered book from the shelf and tucked it behind the other books, where *Little Women* had been. "Next time we come, we'll check the shelf to see if it's been moved too."

Then she quickly signed out *Little Women* for the week and tucked it among the schoolbooks in the hallway. As she walked back into the meeting room, she stopped and scanned the bookshelves again. One book just didn't seem like enough for a whole week. There were so *many* books on the shelves, Innie thought. How could it hurt to take one more home?

She looked around the room. Some girls were milling about, while others were still in the hallway tucking their library books into their coats. After another glance around, Innie darted back to the *A* shelf and helped herself to a second Alcott book, *Little Men.* She quickly carried it to the hallway and hid it under her schoolbooks.

Innie wiped her hands on her skirt, trying to calm down. Surely nobody had seen her. Besides, she wasn't stealing, she was only borrowing. She slipped back to the meeting room, where girls were settling themselves into a circle again.

Just then, a new woman came in. She had dark hair and looked Italian to Innie. The woman made everybody stand and stretch up tall. Then she passed out songbooks, and soon the girls were singing at the top of their lungs. Miss Guerrier stood to one side and smiled.

After the singing, Miss Guerrier led them upstairs to a room where a mirror covered one whole wall, making two of everybody. Miss Guerrier showed a few simple steps to an English country dance, then started the Victrola. Innie stared for a moment as music floated out of the contraption. Then she began following the steps the other girls were making. She had never done this dance before, but she loved it, jumping and kicking and skipping along with the others.

Afterward, Miss Guerrier led everyone back to the second-floor hallway. As the Wednesday afternoon girls pulled on their coats to leave, laughing and chattering, Miss Guerrier spoke to the three newcomers. "Did you enjoy the library club today, girls?"

"Oh, yes, yes," Innie said. What a place this was. A girl could make noise and prance about, and nobody scolded. And that Miss Guerrier was a real lady, Innie decided. She'd just found out about the missing teapot, but she still took the time to smile and make them feel at home.

"We come back next Wednesday," Matela promised.

"I hope to see you sooner," Miss Guerrier said. "Each girl helps out one day a week for an hour or so. 'House time,' we call it. Dusting shelves, checking library cards, packing pottery—we have lots of jobs. Most girls choose Saturdays."

Teresa shook her head. "We can't help on Saturdays. Innie and I have to work in Papà's vegetable stall then. It's his busiest day. But we might be able to come some day after school."

"I too cannot come Saturdays," Matela began. "It is *Shabbos* for us, and we can do no work at all."

"Very well. How does Thursday sound, then? You could help out downstairs, where the pottery and shop are located. Would that work?"

"All three of us, together, on Thursdays?" Innie asked. "We'll have to ask at home because of chores, but I think it'll be all right. Do we start tomorrow?"

"Tomorrow would be lovely. When you arrive, find Miss Brown in the pottery studio. It's on the first floor, in the back." Miss Guerrier smiled and turned toward the kitchen.

Innie pulled her coat from its hook and slung it on. "I'm so glad we can work together," she said, thumping down the stairs to the front door. And while she was helping tomorrow, she might just have a look around, she thought. Maybe she'd find the missing teapot and be a hero. Wouldn't that be grand? "You ready, Teresa? Matela?"

"I am, but . . ." Teresa turned to Matela. "I'm sorry, we can't let my brother Tony see us walking together."

"And why not?" Matela asked. Her pale cheeks flamed, and her dark eyes seemed to grow even darker. "I am not good enough for you?"

"No, no," Innie began. She frowned at Teresa.

Teresa explained. "Papà says we should spend time with Italian girls. If Tony sees us, he'll tell, and maybe Papà won't let us be friends with you."

Innie scowled. "I can do as I like, Matela. I don't have a papa." She threw her arm around Matela's thin shoulders. "I pick my own friends."

Teresa looked as if she might cry. "I want to be friends too, but please, we can't let Tony find out. If we walk

home together, let's step apart before we come to our
tenement. At Luigi's, the butcher's shop. Please."

"All right," Matela said with a serious look on her face.
"My papa, he too is not so happy if I make friends with girls
who aren't Russian and Jewish. So we will keep a secret . . .
and me, I like secrets." She grinned at Innie.

As Innie pulled open the front door, a rainy gust blew
in. Right outside, under a big black umbrella, stood Zio
Giovanni, waiting for them as he always did when it rained.
"That's Uncle," she warned Matela. "We have to go now.
We'll see you tomorrow at house time."

"Oh, Papà," Teresa teased as she stepped out the door.
"Why must you always come with the umbrella? What
am I, salt? Will I melt?"

"No, *bambina.* You're sugar, the sweetest sugar in the
world." He stepped out into the middle of the sidewalk,
shielding both girls with the umbrella.

He didn't call me sugar, Innie realized. *Nobody ever does.
I'm not sweet at all. I'm the salt.*

Rain spattered harder on the umbrella as they started
down the sidewalk. Innie glanced across the street and
saw Matela walking home, all alone. Behind Matela, the
iron gates of Copp's Hill Burying Ground stood open and
dripping in the gray afternoon.

Innie couldn't help but shiver. If there really were ghosts
or *maziks,* this would sure be a good place for them.

CHAPTER 5

HOUSE TIME

It wasn't raining on Thursday, but it might as well have been. A chill April damp blew across the harbor, smelling of fish and salt. Innie hurried up Salem Street, dodging old ladies with grocery sacks and urging Teresa and Matela along. They were heading to the settlement house to do their house time chores, and Innie wanted to get there quickly, before the Thursday girls started their club meeting. "Let's sneak into the meeting room before we start to work. I want to see if anybody messed with that book I hid yesterday."

"Any *mazik,* you mean," Matela said. "Not any*body.*"

"We'll get in trouble," Teresa warned.

"If anybody asks, I'll just say that we're looking for Miss Guerrier so she can show us where to help. Come on, let's hurry."

The settlement house was warm and welcoming. It smelled of hot chocolate and fresh-baked cookies, not salt and fish. Innie hurried upstairs, still wearing her coat. Matela and Teresa followed. Outside the meeting room, a few Thursday girls were whispering together as they hung their coats on the hooks. To Innie, they looked older, thirteen maybe.

Innie led the way into the empty meeting room. At the *A* shelf, she poked her hand behind the neat row of books. She found the hidden book exactly where she'd left it yesterday afternoon.

"What did you expect?" Teresa whispered over Innie's shoulder. "Come on, let's get out of here." The Thursday girls were beginning to wander in. Teresa took Innie's arm and steered her toward the door. "Hurry up. We'll get caught. We're supposed to go and find Miss Brown downstairs."

They made their way down to the first floor, passing other Thursday girls on the stairs. They hurried down the first-floor hallway to the pottery decorating room in the very back.

Innie peered in the doorway. The room looked like an old kitchen. At a long wood table, several older girls, including Carmela, sat with tiny paintbrushes, applying what looked like muddy paint to bowls and plates. At one end of the table, a girl of about fifteen was reading poetry aloud. The painters seemed to be listening intently as they worked. Windows lined the back wall and one side, so that even on a gray day like this, the room was plenty bright.

Some job, Innie thought. No wonder Carmela liked this better than sweating away in a dark, crowded sewing shop with loud machines and a mean boss too.

Miss Brown set down a bowl and walked toward Innie, Matela, and Teresa. "Are you my helpers for today? I've been watching for you. Miss Guerrier said there'd be three."

Innie nodded.

"Welcome to the pottery studio. I'll give you a tour." She smiled and led them back through the hallway to the middle room, which held cupboards and a table. "This is a storage room for our studio, and it's also the eating room for our pottery girls. You may hang your coats here when you come to work. You'll find cleaning supplies in this cupboard."

After hanging their coats, the girls followed Miss Brown to the front room. "This is the shop where we sell our pottery," Miss Brown explained. "You'll dust and sweep to keep it nice for the customers."

Innie looked around, admiring the colorful bowls and plates set out on tables and simple wood shelves. Some of the dishes were plain, but Innie found her eyes drawn to the painted pottery—big vases with flowers, and tiny plates and bowls with funny little chickens and rabbits. Next to the door sat a small table with a notebook and a metal cash box like the one Zio Giovanni used at his vegetable stall.

"Once you've tidied the shop," Miss Brown said, "the rest of your chores will be in the basement. Follow me, please." She led them back through the hall to a narrow door, which opened to a rickety set of steps.

Innie shuddered as they started down. After the bright kitchen and shop, the basement stairs seemed dark and shadowy, with only a thin railing to keep her from pitching over the side. An electric lamp glowed to show the way, but it was so dim that Innie had to step slowly and carefully.

When they reached the bottom, Miss Brown showed them the basement's three rooms. In the very back, under the room where Carmela and her friends painted, was the room where the pottery was made. In the dim light, Innie could make out molds for pottery, barrels filled with clay, and worktables holding bins of tools.

"You won't need to clean in here," Miss Brown said with a laugh. "It will always be filled with clay and mud. But we do try to keep our drying and kiln rooms tidy."

She marched them to the middle room, where tall, open shelves stood against every wall, making the room itself feel crowded. As they walked in, Innie had the oddest sensation. In most basements, a chill dampness seeped right into your bones. She was expecting that here, too, but instead, she felt warmer.

"Here's where we set out the raw pottery to dry before its first firing," Miss Brown explained. "You'll sweep here, but be careful of the shelves. The pottery breaks easily before it's fired." She stepped through the doorway again,

and the girls followed. Nobody had said much except
Miss Brown. As they entered the front room of the basement, Teresa reached out and took Innie's hand. It was
a comfort.

This room felt even warmer than the last. Again, rough
shelves stretched from floor to ceiling, some loaded with
bowls and plates and vases. The front wall had two small
windows high up near the ceiling, but they didn't let in
much light. To one side, Innie saw a brick contraption
with pipes poking out like crooked arms. In the dim light,
it cast strange shadows against the walls.

Miss Brown explained that the brick contraption was
the kiln, or oven, where the pottery was fired twice—once
to make the clay hard, and again to make the painted glazes
shiny. "You'll need to sweep up in here too, girls, but again,
work carefully. These shelves are for decorated pots waiting to go in the kiln for their second firing."

Innie smiled. Now she understood why the basement
was so warm and dry. That kiln was twice as big as Nonna's
cookstove.

Miss Brown showed them brooms and dustpans in a
corner by the kiln, then left them to their work.

"Let's start in the shop and work together," Innie
suggested. That way, nobody would have to sweep alone
in that dark basement.

Upstairs, the girls moved carefully around the shop.
Teresa dusted each piece of pottery, Matela wiped down

the display shelves, and Innie swept the floor. With three girls working, the shop got clean in no time.

In the basement, though, dim light made it difficult to see. Underfoot, the floor felt gritty with bits and pieces of clay and dirt. The girls started in the kiln room. They each grabbed a broom and began to sweep.

As Innie swept a dark corner on the far side of the kiln, she discovered a narrow door no taller than she was. The wood was old and splintery, the knob dark and rusty. "Do you suppose this is the way outside?" she asked Matela. "We could carry out our sweeping dirt if it is." She tried the door. The knob turned, but the door didn't budge.

Matela glanced at the child-sized door. "Probably nobody uses it. Don't worry, over by the shelf I find a rubbish bin."

The girls emptied their dustpans into the bin and moved to the drying room to sweep. When they went back to the kiln room to put their brooms away, Innie tried the little old door again, but it stayed shut.

"This door, I wonder where it goes?"

Matela waved her dustpan toward the door. "Maybe it goes where the *maziks* live," she teased. She was trying to make her voice sound scary, but she only sounded silly. Innie laughed, but Teresa didn't.

"Put your broom away, Innie. Let's get out of this old place," Teresa urged. "We have chores waiting at home."

"Chores, chores," Innie grumbled. "What if I don't want to put my broom away? What if I want to practice my English country dancing instead?"

Innie swung her broom in a circle and twirled around. Then she reached up to sweep spiderwebs from the ceiling and twirled again. She stopped abruptly as her broom bumped something solid, crashing it to the floor.

"Oh, no, Innie, you've done it now," Teresa said.

Innie turned and stared at the pile of sharp, broken clay pieces. She *would* get in trouble, unless she cleaned up the mess really fast. But first she had to get Matela and Teresa out of the room. One person in trouble was bad enough.

"Matela, Teresa, you go back to the middle room and dust again. Pretend we were working in different places."

"But—" Matela began.

"Hurry. I'll clean up this mess, and maybe the ladies won't notice what happened."

Teresa tugged Matela back toward the stairs.

Innie picked up the largest of the broken pieces and dumped them in the bin. She reached for her dustpan and was beginning to sweep when footsteps approached. Innie looked up.

Miss Brown was staring at her from the doorway. "Did I hear a crash?"

Innie's tongue froze. She couldn't speak.

"Have you broken something?"

"I . . . Yes. My broom . . . I bumped . . ."

"Why didn't you fetch me?" Even in the dim light, Innie could tell that Miss Brown was frowning.

"I—I was going to clean up first . . ." Innie began. Her palms went damp with sweat.

"You're the Moretti girl, aren't you? Innie. The cousin. Carmela has mentioned you."

Carmela? What had Carmela told them about her?

"I don't care for this sneaking about," Miss Brown continued. "A proper girl would have come and told me about the breakage right away. Show me which section of the shelf you disturbed."

Innie bent and pointed to a high shelf that held four big vases.

Miss Brown knelt on the basement floor. "Oh, my. You've broken one of our largest pots. Those chrysanthemum vases take hours of work. And they sell for fifty dollars in the shop. Mercy."

"I'm very sorry." Innie could barely squeeze the words out. She'd gotten in trouble before, lots of times. But she'd never gotten in fifty dollars' worth. That was a fortune.

"You *should* be sorry. Have you anything else to confess?"

"Pardon?"

"A girl who misbehaves once will misbehave again. Tell me, Innie, do you know anything about Miss Guerrier's missing teapot?"

The teapot? Miss Brown thought she'd taken the teapot too! Innie's stomach twisted into a hard knot. "No. I . . . I don't know anything about it. Except what I heard when you were . . . talking."

"Yes. I noticed you eavesdropping. You have *nothing* more to tell me?"

"No, Miss. Please. I broke the vase, but that's all."

"Well, that's certainly enough. I shall be keeping an eye on you."

"Yes, Miss."

Miss Brown strode away. As her footsteps faded, Innie bent and swept the last of the clay pieces into the dustpan. She dumped the debris into the bin, wishing it were large enough that she could crawl in herself and hide. Miss Brown didn't like her. She'd be watching everything Innie did from now on. And if she were like most adults, she'd find plenty to grumble about.

Innie set her broom against the basement wall, willing herself not to cry. As she started upstairs, Teresa and Matela each tried to put an arm around her, but Innie shrugged them off.

"Oh, Innie," Teresa began.

"Don't you start," Innie said. "I've had enough scolding already."

"We don't scold," Matela said softly. "We are your friends. That Miss Brown, she is wrong about you."

They'd listened. They'd heard everything, Innie realized.

She hadn't thought that she could feel worse than when Miss Brown had been accusing her, but now, knowing Teresa and Matela had heard, waves of shame washed over her. Her face burned.

"I don't want to talk about it," Innie said. "Let's just go home."

⚜

Later that evening, after the lodgers had been fed and the dishes were washed and dried, Innie went upstairs to visit Teresa. Innie's ears still stung from Miss Brown's words, and Teresa had a soft heart. Innie needed a bucketful of sympathy.

At the kitchen table upstairs, Zio Giovanni had his cash box open and was counting out money while Zia Rachela wrote down numbers in her book. That was bad news for Innie. It meant Carmela couldn't spread out all her books and study in the kitchen tonight.

Sure enough, when Innie got to the bedroom that her cousins shared, both girls were there, sitting on the bed. Carmela was surrounded by books, and she was frowning.

I picked a bad time, Innie thought. *Carmela's always a grump when she's studying to be a citizen.*

"And what do you want, Innie? Foolishness? Making trouble again? I don't have time for it."

"But, Carmela—" Teresa began.

"What? You think I buy extra lamp oil for you two babies to see by? I've got books and books to read."

Innie sighed. "I just wanted to talk to Teresa," she said. "There was nothing to do downstairs."

"Nothing to do? I'll tell Nonna you said so. She'll find you something. Scrubbing or sweeping."

Sweeping again. Innie never wanted to hold another broom as long as she lived. She hoped Carmela wouldn't hear about the broken vase.

"Come on, Carmela," Teresa interrupted. "We worked hard today."

"Hard? You want to know hard? The Bill of Rights, that's hard." Carmela waved a thick blue book under Teresa's nose.

"What is it?" Innie asked. "What's the Bill of Rights?" If Carmela got to talking about her citizen hearing, maybe she wouldn't go poking into Innie's troubles.

"Here in America they got a whole string of rules. The government, politics, democracy, who can do what. Very confusing."

"The judge can ask all that?" Innie asked. "At the hearing?"

"The judge can ask what he wants." Carmela waved her hands. "The Bill of Rights, the Constitution, all the presidents. When I go for my citizen hearing, I gotta know *everything*, or else that judge won't let me be American. I heard he's turned down other Italians."

"The Yankee ladies like you at the pottery," Teresa said. "So why won't the judge like you for a citizen? When you're not bossing us, you're a nice person."

"The ladies took me at the pottery because I can paint. To be American, I gotta know the rules. It's not about being a nice person."

"I don't get it," Innie said. "I'm American, and I don't know all those rules. How come *you* have to study them?"

"You got lucky," Carmela explained. "You and Teresa got born here so you're already American. They'll pound the rules into your head in school. But me, I'm born in Italy, so I gotta have that hearing. And how am I gonna do that with all this chitter-chatter? Innie, Teresa, go bother somebody else."

"But, Carmela—" Innie began.

Carmela frowned. "You watch that back-talking, Innocenza Moretti. Bad enough at home, but I don't want you getting in trouble at the settlement house. I got you in there, and if you make trouble, they'll blame me."

So Carmela didn't know yet. Innie hoped it stayed that way.

"You hush now," Carmela continued. "I have to study. And remember, no trouble at the settlement house. Or else."

Too late for that, Innie thought.

"Come on," Teresa said. "Let's go sit in the kitchen."

"Not the kitchen," Innie said. She couldn't talk to

Teresa about the trouble with Miss Brown in front of her aunt and uncle. That would just lead to more scoldings.

"The roof will be cold. You want to sit on the stairs?" Teresa asked.

Innie shrugged. "It stinks on the stairs. Old lady Napoli burned her supper again, and the privy smells from the cellar are bad. I'll go downstairs and read that book I borrowed."

If only it were summer, Innie grumbled to herself as she tromped downstairs. In the summer, a person could climb to the roof or sit out on the stoop if she wanted to be by herself or talk privately with someone. But on cold, damp days, it was hard to find a quiet spot.

And in Boston, damp days, like troubles, came all too often.

CHAPTER 6
TWO PERFECT FLAMES

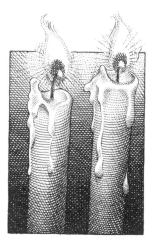

By Sunday morning, as Innie dressed for church, she had almost forgotten Miss Brown's unkind words. She and Nonna were up early so that Nonna could light candles and pray to the Holy Mother before Mass started.

"Sit still, you," Nonna said. She buttoned up the back of Innie's dress and ran a stiff brush through Innie's tangled hair. Then she twisted it into a single long, smooth braid, her old fingers moving slowly.

Sitting still wasn't easy, but Innie liked the feel of the heavy braid on her back and the crispness of her clean, just-ironed dress. She closed her eyes and imagined that maybe someday she'd look as nice as Carmela. If that ever happened, Nonna would sure be proud of her.

"You gonna run on the streets today again?" Nonna asked. "You gonna spoil this fancy braiding?"

"I'll try not to," Innie said. She knew Nonna always

took extra care on Sundays so they'd look their best. She'd try hard today.

Outside on the sidewalk, Innie took slow, careful steps and gave her grandmother her arm to lean on for the short walk to Saint Leonard's. This early, the streets were quiet, with only the occasional slam of a door or baby's cry sounding from a nearby flat. Pigeons pecked among the debris. A damp gray mist hovered about the shops and tenements, softening the edges of the buildings.

At the church door, a cluster of Sisters in their dark robes were entering. Innie slowed even more so that by the time she'd helped Nonna to the church door, the Sisters had disappeared inside.

At the back of the church, Nonna dipped her fingers in the holy water, faced the altar, and crossed herself. Innie did the same, and then followed her grandmother up the right aisle to the statue of the Holy Mother. Only a few candles burned, and the quiet church felt dark and holy.

Innie knelt next to her grandmother in front of the statue. Nonna pressed coins into Innie's hand. Innie dropped the coins into the box and said a prayer to the Holy Mother in heaven as she lit a candle for Mama. Then she lit a second candle and prayed for Papà's soul. She stared at the two perfect flames. Her parents must have been like those flames, Innie thought. Warm and shining and beautiful.

She wondered if Papà had looked like Zio Giovanni, his older brother. And had Mama been thin, like Innie herself? So much she didn't know. So much she prayed for—a picture, a voice, a memory, anything. But all Innie could see were golden flames and soft gray smoke.

A sudden thought made her fold her hands tighter and begin another prayer. Mama and Papà wouldn't like it that Innie had broken that big vase. She prayed that she wouldn't get in more trouble at the settlement house, prayed that wherever they were, Mama and Papà didn't know Innie was in trouble again. Or if they did, that they'd soon forgive her.

At her side, Nonna dropped coins in the box and lit her candles. Two wet lines tracked down Nonna's wrinkled cheeks as she murmured, asking the Holy Mother to watch over the souls of her son Giuseppe and his wife, Serafina. She prayed for all the people hurt and killed in the Chelsea fire and for all the families left behind.

Innie held her breath, for she knew what was coming next, and it always made her stomach churn. Sure enough, in Nonna's slow, creaky whisper, Innie heard the words . . .

"And please, Holy Mary, Mother of God, watch over the orphan child Innocenza. Guide her to your holy ways, for she is yours, promised to you now and forever. In the name of the Father, the Son, and the Holy Ghost. Amen."

As Nonna finished, a Sister knelt at Innie's side, as if Nonna's words had called her. Innie squeezed her eyes shut and silently added one more prayer to her list. "Please, Holy Mother. The promise—I can't. Don't make me."

It was a relief to stand up and lead Nonna to the pew. Innie watched as the women and girls of the North End drifted into church in little clumps, the women in black, wearing shawls, and the girls bright in their best dresses. Soon Teresa, Carmela, and Zia Rachela joined them. Teresa reached out and squeezed Innie's hand as she sat down. "You and Nonna been here a long time?"

"Long enough."

"Sore knees?"

Innie rolled her eyes. "So much kneeling, I got blisters."

Teresa hid a giggle behind her hand.

Making a joke helped. Innie had never told her cousin about the prayer that Nonna always said when she lit those candles. Nobody in the family knew about the promising. *This is between me and you and the Holy Mother,* Nonna always said, and Innie had kept it secret too—she couldn't bear to tell anyone.

⚜

On Monday afternoon, Innie and Teresa were working arithmetic problems at Teresa's kitchen table when Carmela came home from work, looking as if she'd eaten a whole batch of spicy peppers. Her cheeks flamed, and she threw down her coat.

"What's wrong, Carmela?" Teresa asked.

"What isn't wrong?" she shot back. "Someone's stealing again at the pottery."

Innie's stomach lurched.

"What's missing?" Teresa asked. "Tell us everything."

Carmela's hand gripped the back of one of the chairs. "Last week Miss Guerrier's teapot went missing. It was solid silver and very old, from her mother's family."

"We heard," Teresa said.

And Miss Brown thinks I took it, Innie thought.

"Now a pottery set is gone," Carmela continued. "And a new wool shawl that belongs to one of the girls. The thief must be stealing things and selling them somewhere."

Innie felt cold. Would Miss Brown think she'd done this too? She studied Carmela's face. "What's in a pottery set?"

Carmela looked angry. "This was a baby set—a set I painted—with a plate, a bowl, and a mug. A customer ordered it special. She wanted little rabbits and the name *Margaret.* I did a nice job on that set. Miss Brown opened the kiln on Saturday and took out the finished pottery, but this morning the baby set was missing."

"Are you sure?" Innie began.

Carmela waved her hands. "We looked everywhere. And tomorrow, the rich Yankee lady who ordered the set, she'll come to the shop and we won't have her pottery and she'll complain. And me, I've got that citizen hearing to study for and my mind is so stirred up I can't think."

Carmela stormed from the kitchen and marched out into the hall. A door slammed, and Innie was sure she saw the kitchen wall shake. She shivered.

Teresa spoke softly. "They can't blame you this time, Innie. You haven't been anywhere near the settlement house since Thursday." She stopped to take a deep breath. "Could Matela be right? Could it be a ghost? A *mazik?*" Teresa's cheeks had gone pale.

Innie swallowed. "I don't know, Teresa. But you're right about one thing. This time, I don't have anything to do with the trouble. That's a nice change, isn't it?"

All afternoon and during supper, the new thefts nagged at Innie. She wanted to help those ladies find out who was stealing. So after supper she went upstairs again and pushed open the door to her cousins' room. Carmela was using some more of her precious lamp oil. She'd taken possession of the bed again, filling every inch with books and papers. Teresa sat on a chair in the corner, reading a book from the settlement house.

As Innie walked in, Carmela looked up and scowled. "Go away, Innie. Can't you see I'm studying?"

"But I have an idea." Innie stepped closer to the bed. "I think I know how somebody might get into the settlement house and steal things."

"Stay out of it, Innie. The ladies are taking care of it," Carmela said. "The last thing we need is you getting in the middle of all this."

But I'm already in the middle of it, Innie thought. She opened her mouth to protest, but Carmela cut her off.

"Look, you. I have to learn the three branches of government tonight if I'm ever gonna be American. So go away."

Go away. Like I don't belong here, not even a little, Innie fumed. Sometimes Carmela made her so mad. "I'm already an American, so there."

"Sure, you're a big shot. Innocenza Maria Moretti. That sounds real American to me. A regular Yankee." Carmela poked Innie's arm. "Look at you. Long dark hair, little gold earrings. You're born here, but you're still Italian. You'll always be Italian."

Innie's hands flew to her hair—she couldn't do much about that. But one thing she *could* fix. With trembling fingers, she opened the gold hoops at her ears and slipped them out. "There. Not so Italian now."

"Innie, don't," Teresa said. "Put your earrings back in."

"No. Why should I? I want to look American, and American girls don't wear earrings." She stuck the gold hoops into her pocket.

Carmela sighed. "Put them back in, Innie. Your mother, she's the one who pierced your ears. Wear the earrings for her."

"I don't even remember my mother. And wherever she is, she sure doesn't care about earrings anymore." Innie turned and slammed out of the room before Carmela or Teresa could say a word. She ran smack into Zia Rachela.

"I see Carmela's temper is still smoking," her aunt said. She led Innie into the kitchen and nudged her into a chair. "She studies too hard, that one. Don't let her take it out on you." She gave Innie's shoulder a squeeze.

Innie leaned her elbow on the table and rested her chin in her hand. It felt nice to sit in the warm kitchen with Zia Rachela. "Carmela, she's always bossing us around. I'm not even her sister and she tells me what to do."

Her aunt laughed. "Ah, the oldest daughter. My sister was like that too. But Carmela will relax soon, when the citizen hearing is over."

"Is the hearing soon?" Innie had the feeling she should stay miles away from Carmela until it was over.

"Soon enough. She wants very much to make a citizen. That, even I can understand." A soft, sad look crossed her face.

"What do you mean, Zia Rachela?"

"In Italy, I belonged. Here I am a stranger. If Carmela makes a citizen, then she will belong to America. She will feel right here."

"And you don't?" *How can that be?* Innie wondered. *Zia Rachela is the heart and soul of her family. If she doesn't belong here, nobody does.*

Zia Rachela shrugged. "Mostly I feel fine. Here in the North End, with Italians all around, I might as well still be living in the village. But sometimes, around the Yankees, I feel so foreign. I wish . . ."

"What?"

"Oh, nothing, *bambina.*" She smoothed Innie's hair with a gentle hand.

Zia Rachela made wishes too? Her aunt wanted things she didn't have? Innie would never have guessed such a thing. Her own biggest wish tonight was that things would go well at the settlement house from now on. That there'd be no more stealing and no more trouble.

⚜

But on Wednesday afternoon as the library club meeting began, Miss Guerrier sat stiff in her chair and looked at the girls without smiling. "I have an unfortunate announcement. Last week a silver teapot and a crate of food were taken from the settlement house. Then some pottery and a shawl disappeared. Now food has been taken from the club kitchen." Miss Guerrier looked around the room, and her gaze came to rest on Innie.

Innie tried to breathe, but her lungs felt stiff. She pinched the blue cloth of her dress. Surely the lady knew that Innie had been nowhere near the settlement house for almost a week.

"Girls, please. We need your cooperation. Because the settlement house is a place for girls, we are quite careful about who is allowed to enter the building. As far as we can determine, we have had no strangers coming and going. That means the person responsible for the missing items may, in fact, be a member of one of the library clubs."

A shocked silence followed Miss Guerrier's words. Innie couldn't help scanning the faces of the girls closest to her. She felt eyes on her own face as well and knew that every girl in the room was asking herself the same question. *Who? Who could it be?*

Miss Guerrier cleared her throat. "One moment, and then we'll return to Tom Canty and the Prince of Wales. If any of you have information, if you see or hear anything that pertains to the missing items, please speak to Miss Brown or me in private. Thank you."

As Miss Guerrier opened the book and began to read aloud, Innie caught sight of Maria and Stella from her class at school. They were staring at her as if they thought she was guilty and they'd love to tattle to Miss Guerrier just as they tattled to the teachers.

Innie turned her face away from Maria and Stella and tried to concentrate on Miss Guerrier's voice. Soon the words of the story carried her away to long-ago England.

At borrowing time, Innie scanned Miss Alcott's books and selected a new one. No more sneaking extra books, she decided. She was glad she'd brought both of last week's books to return. She'd finished them both by hiding them between her schoolbooks and reading when the teacher wasn't looking. Quickly, she slipped *Little Men* back onto the shelf where it belonged.

After book borrowing and singing, Miss Guerrier gathered the girls together. "We have some work to do, and I'm hoping you'll enjoy helping. Follow me, please."

Innie let her hand slide along the smooth banister, remembering her ride, as they climbed the long staircase. The string of girls trooped past the third floor, all the way up to the top floor, where the ladies had their apartment. But Miss Guerrier told the girls to keep climbing.

"Ah, here we are. Step carefully, please." She opened a skinny door and led the way out onto a flat, sunny wooden terrace that covered the whole roof. A breeze caught Innie's hair.

This roof was twice as big as theirs at home, Innie thought. She admired the brick walls built partway up the sides, which made the terrace feel like an outdoor room. She darted forward and checked the views. The settlement house sat at the very top of the hill, so she could see the big buildings of Boston on her right. On her left, the harbor stretched out, with Cambridge and Charlestown beyond. *It's so beautiful, I'd move my bed up here if I lived in such a house,* she thought.

Miss Guerrier was wearing a large apron, and from the pockets she pulled out several brown sacks. "You'll notice

that the Monday and Tuesday girls have been busy," she
began. "They've hauled up soil and filled our planting
boxes." She pointed toward rows of long, narrow wooden
boxes along each side of the roof. "Your job will be the
planting. If you'll arrange yourselves into small groups,
I'll hand out the seeds."

Innie, Teresa, and Matela stood close together.

"Sweet peas for you?" Miss Guerrier asked politely.

"What is this, please?" Matela asked.

Miss Guerrier handed her a white envelope. "They're
flowers. You'll need to plant them there, in the north
corner, where we've strung up the strings, for they love
to climb." After Miss Guerrier had given out all her seeds,
she bustled from group to group with advice.

"This planting on the roof, it's a good idea," Matela
said. "I will tell Mama and Papa."

Innie smiled. "Nonna grows vegetables in window
boxes and on our roof too. She says American tomatoes
don't taste like Italian tomatoes, so she grows her own.
Beans, lettuce, lots of vegetables. Flowers too. But I don't
think she has sweet peas."

"My family, too, can make a garden in boxes," Matela
said. "Mama will love it. My papa, he buys his eggs from
a farmer. We can ask the farmer for dirt."

Innie felt a grin break out across her face. "And, Teresa,
we can surprise Nonna. We can plant those sweet peas."

"I'll ask Miss Guerrier where to get the seeds," Teresa

volunteered. She brushed off her dirty fingers and hurried across the roof.

Curious, Innie turned to Matela. "How come you buy eggs from a farmer, instead of from a shop or the market?"

"My papa, he *is* the shop for our people. He buys eggs from the farmer and sells to the neighbors. Good eggs, only the freshest. And I help. Every night my brothers and me, we candle the day's eggs and set them into boxes."

"What do you mean?"

Matela raised her fingers as if holding an egg, then brought the pretend egg close and peered at it. "A candle behind the egg, it shines light through. So we see spots. Eggs with spots, we can't use."

"I don't understand," Innie said.

Matela chewed her bottom lip. "Spots . . . How to explain? Some eggs will grow into chickens, some will not. We Jews eat only the eggs which will not."

"I still don't understand."

"When you crack an egg, do you ever see a blood spot—a little speck of red?"

Innie nodded. "Nonna scoops it out with a spoon."

Matela shook her head. "We can't do that. To obey Jewish food laws, we must throw away the whole egg. So my brothers and me, we candle the eggs first to make sure they are pure. Even so, the women must look closely when they cook."

"What are Jewish food laws?" Innie had never heard of such a thing.

"Rules. What we may eat and what we may not. You are Christian. Do you not have rules?"

"I guess." Innie thought for a moment. "No meat on Fridays. Special strict rules during Lent."

"For us, Passover is strict. Not so different, then."

Innie shook her head. Worrying about spots in eggs still seemed odd. She wouldn't say it aloud, but being Jewish seemed about as different from being Catholic as a person could get.

Teresa returned, holding tight to the envelope that had held the sweet pea seeds. "Miss Guerrier wrote down where to buy the seeds. Do you think Papà will give us the money?"

"He will if *you* ask him," Innie said. "He never says no to you."

Matela smiled. "Papas. They're always soft for their daughters."

Innie turned away. Talk like that made her eyes burn. She blinked hard. Maybe Catholic or Jewish wasn't the big difference after all; maybe it was girls with fathers and girls without.

CHAPTER 7

THE MARGARET MUG

On Thursday, Innie and Teresa waited after school for Matela. Together they climbed Salem Street, trudging through another damp April afternoon.

"You think that sun's mad with us?" Matela asked. "Gray everywhere. Makes me grumpy."

"You know what makes *me* grumpy?" Innie said. She ran her fingertips along the cold, rough bricks of a building. "Somebody is causing trouble at the settlement house. It's not right. We've got to do something."

"What, scare away the *mazik*?" Matela knocked on her head with one hand. "I'm thinking and thinking, but I don't know how."

"I'm going to do more than clean today," Innie said. "I'll poke into every corner. Miss Brown found the missing food crate down in the basement. We might find something too."

"Good idea," Matela agreed. "The ladies will think we're the best cleaners."

Innie nodded. "But instead we'll be the best snoopers."

"No dark corners for me," Teresa said. "I'll snoop in the shop."

At the settlement house, the shop shelves had grown more crowded with newly finished pottery. Cleaning took longer than it had the week before, and the girls examined each plate, bowl, and cup on the chance that the missing set might have just been misplaced.

"Could this be the baby set that's missing?" Matela asked, holding up a small, cream-colored mug. "It has rabbits like your sister painted."

Innie stepped closer and examined the bowl and plate. Little blue rabbits danced along the edges, but the name painted in fancy letters on the dishes was *Barbara,* not *Margaret.* "This Barbara, she's really lucky," Innie said. "Imagine, somebody having enough money they could buy a fancy dish for a tiny little girl."

"Look here," Teresa said. She opened what looked like a small notebook. "Here's a list of what's been sold, right next to the money box. A blue vase. A big green plate. A whole batch of dishes."

As Innie swept the floor, she found crates stacked under the tables. She set her broom aside and opened the crates, but they only held old newspapers, probably used for wrapping up dishes that customers wanted to carry home.

As hard as they looked, the girls could find nothing in the shop that seemed out of place. Downstairs in the basement, they swept up the drying room first. Again they found nothing suspicious.

In the kiln room, Innie checked the old door in the corner. It looked just as it had the last time—dirty, splintery, and shut tight.

"Come on, Innie, move that broom. Matela and I are doing all the sweeping," Teresa complained. "It's so dirty over here by the kiln. Looks like our kitchen floor after my brothers finish eating."

"What do you mean?" Innie joined her cousin beside the kiln and stooped to study the floor. "Stop sweeping for a minute."

Matela joined them. "What is it?"

Innie picked up the dustpan. "Sweep the dirt in here, Teresa. We'll take it to better light."

The three girls crowded under the bare electric bulb, studying the contents of the dustpan. Innie stirred it lightly with one finger, finding pale crumbs and broken walnut shells amid the bits of clay and ordinary dirt. She picked up a crumb and pinched it between her fingers. "This looks like those nice cookies Miss Guerrier gave us," she said. "And there were walnuts missing from that crate."

"How do these things come here?" Matela poked at the walnut shells.

"That's easy. The thief was here. He cracked nuts.

He carried cookies down from the kitchen and ate them. But who is he?"

"Yes," Matela began. "That's the hard part—who? Do we tell Miss Guerrier what we find here?"

"Not yet. Let's sweep some more. See if we find anything else." Innie swept carefully all around the old door. Matela checked the pottery shelves while Teresa swept the side near the kiln.

"Find more crumbs or shells?" Innie asked. "I didn't."

"Not me," Matela said.

"They just seemed to be here, by the kiln," Teresa said.

After putting away the brooms and dustpans, Innie walked once more around the kiln room, peering into every shadowy corner and running her fingers along each shelf. There were no more crumbs or shells, and nothing else out of the ordinary.

Matela and Teresa walked ahead of her into the shadowy hallway and started up the stairs. Innie put her hand on the railing to follow, then stopped. *There's one place we didn't check,* she thought. *Under the stairs.*

She moved alongside the stairway. Above, she could hear the scrape of the girls' feet as they climbed the steps.

"Innie?" Matela asked. "You coming?"

"Go on. I'll just be a minute," Innie said. She ducked under the stairway. Cobwebs stuck to her fingers as she felt along the wood that held up the steps. Her foot nudged something. Swallowing hard, she bent and brushed the floor, hoping there were no mice. Her fingers bumped into a wooden block that supported a post. Wood. All she'd kicked was a piece of wood. Above, she heard the door shut with a squeak and a click.

Innie pulled back her hand and wiped it on her skirt. She squinted, trying to see farther into the shadows. What was that, over there on the floor to the left? She reached out and felt a cool, round shape, something with a handle. Could it be a silver teapot? No, it was only a piece of pottery, a small mug. Part of the missing baby set? *I knew I'd find something,* she thought, smiling. She felt around for a plate and bowl but found only dust and cobwebs.

Clutching the mug in one hand, she pounded up the steps two at a time. At the top, she flung open the door and held the mug out. "Teresa, Matela, look what I've got!"

But the face that stared back at Innie didn't belong to her cousin or her friend. Neither did the voice.

"Yes. Look what you've got."

Miss Brown was staring at her with a frown on her face and a pair of blue eyes so icy, they made the raw wind off the harbor feel like a summer breeze.

Innie took a step backward, but her foot found air. If only those rickety stairs would swallow her up, she thought, but they wouldn't. So she squared her shoulders and stepped forward toward Miss Brown and a big pile of trouble.

⌘

Minutes later Innie was sitting at the kitchen table
surrounded by three angry faces. On one side of her sat
Miss Brown, on the other, Miss Guerrier. At the end of
the table, Carmela sat so stiff, Innie wasn't sure her cousin
was even breathing. The Margaret mug sat in the middle
of the table, blue rabbits dancing on pale, creamy pottery.
Innie had never felt less like dancing in her life.

"Where did you find the mug, Innie?" Miss Brown
began.

"In the basement. Under the stairs."

Carmela sniffed and scowled even more ferociously.

"And what were you doing under the basement stairs?"
Miss Guerrier asked.

Innie looked down at her hands. They were smudged
and dirty. She twisted her fingers together. "Snooping."

"I beg your pardon?" Innie wasn't sure which lady had
said that.

"I was snooping," she repeated in a small voice. She
hesitated—she didn't want to get Teresa and Matela in
trouble too. "It was all my idea. I was trying to find the
thief. Or at least a clue."

"Did you find anything besides the mug?" Miss Brown
continued.

"A little," Innie said. "Teresa was sweeping by the kiln.
She found walnut shells and cookie crumbs."

"Where else did you . . . er . . . snoop?" Miss Brown
asked.

"All around the basement." Sweat began to gather along her sides. "We also . . . Well, we *cleaned* the shop really well."

"Meaning you searched it?" Miss Brown's eyes hadn't warmed up.

"Yes. We . . . we looked at every pot and in all the crates. We were just trying to help . . ."

"I see." Miss Brown stopped talking and nodded to Miss Guerrier. "You didn't break anything today and *forget* to tell us, did you?"

"No, Miss." Innie didn't dare look at Carmela.

"Innie," Miss Guerrier said. "What you're telling us could be true."

At that, Innie took a deep breath. Maybe she wasn't in trouble after all. Maybe they just wanted to know what she'd found out. She wished she had more to tell.

"But I have my doubts," Miss Guerrier added. "I seem to remember catching you on the stairs the day we were moving in."

"The day the silver teapot disappeared from our *upstairs* apartment," Miss Brown added. "I also thought I saw someone poking about in the kitchen that afternoon. Was it you?"

Innie nodded. Her cheeks burned and she tried to take a breath.

"I've had a disturbing report about you as well," Miss Guerrier said. "From one of the other Wednesday afternoon girls."

The breath that Innie had taken went cold in her chest. Maria and Stella. They'd snitched. But what had they seen?

Miss Guerrier's face looked as stiff and starched as her collar. "One of the girls saw you hide a book in the hallway last week. That's very disturbing. The books are for everyone. If a girl steals them, we won't have enough to go around."

Last week, last week . . . Innie tried to guess what those tattletales might have seen. "I—I didn't steal. I borrowed. I signed out my book, just like the other girls. I wrote my name on a card and gave it to the older girl who was collecting them. You can check the cards."

Innie folded her hands under the table, hoping Miss Guerrier couldn't read her mind, hoping Maria and Stella hadn't seen her with two books, but with only one. *Holy Mother, please help me. I won't do that anymore, I promise. I won't take out a book without signing the card. Only please, don't let them blame me for all this trouble,* she prayed.

Miss Guerrier frowned, but it wasn't so much an angry frown as a confused one. "I will check the cards. But, Innie, if you weren't stealing, why did you hide the book?"

This might work. Innie looked to the end of the table. She hoped she wouldn't get Carmela in trouble, but she had to try to explain. She had no other choice. "Carmela, she told Teresa and me to hide our library books. Zio Giovanni, he thinks we come here to learn sewing. If he finds out about the library books, he won't let us come."

Miss Guerrier stared at Innie for a minute, then turned to Carmela. "Is this true? You told her to hide her books?"

"Yes." Carmela's voice sounded scratchy. "Papà's old-fashioned. Girls shouldn't waste time reading books, he says. It keeps us from doing what really matters, which is helping Mama and Nonna take care of our family."

"I see. That casts a new light on this matter, then. Thank you, Carmela."

Both ladies stood and stepped out of the room. Through the kitchen door, Innie could hear them whispering together. She kept her eyes on the table, so she wouldn't have to look at Carmela.

When the ladies returned, Miss Guerrier spoke in a serious voice. "If we have accused you unfairly, Innie, we're sorry. But we will be keeping a watch on you. You, your cousin Teresa, and the Rosen girl are all new to the library club. And we had no trouble until you three joined us. You, in particular, have misbehaved. You broke a valuable vase and tried to hide the evidence. You have been seen in places where you should not have been. Today, a missing mug shows up in your hands. So it's only natural for us to be suspicious."

Innie chewed on her bottom lip and tried to keep from crying.

Miss Guerrier kept talking. "You'll want to behave quite properly from now on. You won't want to do anything that places you under suspicion. Do you understand? We're giving you a warning. If one more thing goes wrong, or if we find you in questionable circumstances again, you won't be allowed to attend the library club. Have I made myself clear?"

Innie thought back over the two club meetings—the books, the singing, the folk dancing. And that garden on the roof—she had to belong to this club so she could watch those sweet peas start to climb their strings. She nodded to Miss Guerrier. "Yes, ma'am. I'll be good. I promise."

The two ladies left, closing the kitchen door behind them. Carmela stood and walked to Innie's end of the table. "How *could* you, Innie? You've shamed me. Shamed the whole family."

"I *didn't* steal, Carmela. I'm innocent."

"Ha! The only thing innocent about you is your name. *Innocenza*—what a joke!" Carmela scowled. "Look, you, Teresa told me you've been sneaking extra books. That's dumb. If you finish your book before the week's over, all you have to do is bring it back and sign out a new one. You're just lucky they didn't catch that."

"But, Carmela . . ."

"Hush. Listen to me. One more mistake and you're kicked out. I could lose my job. With no job, the judge, he might not want me for a citizen." Carmela poked her sharp fingernail into Innie's shoulder, and fire flashed in her dark eyes. "So you, Innocenza Maria Moretti, be good. I know, you don't have much practice with good, but you're smart. You learn it, or else."

❧

"What? What did they say? What happened?" Matela and Teresa had been waiting on the front steps, and they peppered Innie with questions as she rushed outside.

For once the cold air felt good; the dampness took away some of the fire in Innie's cheeks. "They think I'm the thief—they blamed me." Her voice wavered, and she swallowed back tears.

"That's not fair," Teresa said. "Come, let's go walk by the water and you can tell us everything."

"Everything," Matela agreed.

They turned toward the harbor. As Innie spilled out her story, she felt arms come around her from both sides.

"Even Carmela yelled at you," Teresa grumbled. "I'm not speaking to her for a week."

"You told Carmela about the extra book, Teresa."

"Innie, I'm sorry. I didn't mean to. I won't tell her *anything* now. I'm not speaking to her."

"Those ladies are not fair," Matela said loudly. "Innie, you don't take anything. You borrow an extra book, yes, but for the rest, you are trying to help. Why don't those

Yankee ladies understand?" She hugged Innie tighter. "I think it's a *mazik* making trouble."

"Matela's right," Teresa said. "It could be a ghost or a *mazik*."

It felt good to have Teresa and Matela on her side. But Innie shook her head. What they said didn't quite make sense. "Do ghosts get hungry? Do *maziks* leave crumbs and walnut shells? No. It has to be a real person."

"What do you know of *maziks*?" Matela demanded. She stood and pointed at a small boat in the harbor. "*Maziks,* they can sit anywhere. In a tree, on a chimney, right there in that boat. And they slip in and out of doors, even with locks on. They like to play tricks. They might make crumbs just for mischief—who can say?"

"Come on," Innie said. "*Maziks* aren't real." But still, the damp air made her shiver.

"*I* know," Matela said. "We'll prove Innie doesn't make the trouble. We'll prove it's a *mazik*."

"How could we do that?" Innie demanded.

Nobody spoke for a minute. Matela chewed on her bottom lip. "I don't know yet. But I will think of something. Tonight, when it gets dark . . ." She paused and looked out over the water, as if the answer might be hiding under its choppy surface.

"What, Matela?" Teresa asked. "What about tonight?"

"We sneak out to the burying ground. From there we watch the house."

"I thought you said we couldn't see a *mazik*," Innie grumbled. "So why watch?"

"The *mazik*, you can't see. But what he does, you might see that. If we watch the house after all the club girls leave, we might see the mischief."

"Sneaking out at night? Oh, Matela. We can't even think such a thing," Teresa said. "Mama and Papà don't let Carmela out alone at night, and she's grown. One of my brothers always walks with her. We can't come out at night. We'd get in terrible trouble."

"Innie is already in terrible trouble. We must help her," Matela said.

Innie swallowed hard. Come to the burying ground in the dark? Even she wasn't sure she could do it. But if Matela was a good enough friend to think up such an idea, she'd find the courage somewhere. Besides, Innie thought, there was just the tiniest chance that Matela's plan might really help them discover the culprit.

Innie took a deep breath. "All right. We'll do it," she said. "But I won't be looking for *maziks* or ghosts. I'll be watching for a human troublemaker. I want to catch that thief so he doesn't keep getting me in trouble."

empty and silent. The burying ground was only a few steps beyond. The iron gates hung open, casting huge shadows on the street.

As the girls approached, a moaning sound drifted out from behind the gates. Teresa grabbed Innie's hand. Innie held on hard, and her heart thumped fast. The moaning came again, nearer. *Hoooo. Hoooooo.*

"We can't go in there," Teresa began.

"Ha! Just me!" Matela jumped from behind the gates, waving her arms.

Innie's breath came out in a whoosh. She tried to laugh, but it sounded squeaky. Her heartbeat wouldn't settle down. "Have you been waiting long?"

"Not very. But I'm glad you're here. The Thursday night girls, they come out soon, I think."

"At nine o'clock," Teresa answered with a tremble in her voice. "How could you wait here alone, Matela? We should have planned to meet at the church."

"Me? A church? I cannot stand by a church."

"Why not?" Innie asked. She'd feel a lot safer standing on the steps of Old North than at the gates of the burying ground just now.

"On every church I see a cross. I am more safe with the dead people."

A shiver crawled up and down Innie's back.

"What's wrong with crosses?" Teresa whispered. "I don't understand."

CHAPTER 8
NIGHT WATCH

"Hurry, Teresa," Innie whispered. "Matela's waiting for us by now. We can't leave her in the burying ground all by herself at night . . ."

She tugged her cousin's hand, pulling her from shadow to shadow along the dark alleyway. A few men and older boys were still out on Salem Street, so Innie and Teresa had to creep up the hill through the narrow alleys, away from the gaslights.

"Oh, Innie. We're being so wicked. If Mama and Papà find out . . ."

"Everybody's asleep. Besides, if they find out, you just say *I* made you come. They'll blame *me*, not you."

As they passed the back door of a bakery, they heard a skittering sound nearby. Innie walked faster, trying not to imagine the hungry rat who'd made the noise. At last they reached Hull Street and the Old North Church. Up here, away from the shops and cafés, the street stood

"Back in Russia, the soldiers ride into our villages on big black horses. In one hand, they carry a sword. Around their neck, they wear a cross." Matela scratched at one of the stones in the wall, then went on. "And every time the soldiers come, it is bad for us. After, someone is always crying."

Those soldiers . . . Innie didn't want to think about such a thing.

"Come, let's hide quick. Those Thursday girls come out soon." Matela hurried them inside the iron gates and led them along a row of crooked gravestones. Innie tried to walk between the graves, not on top of any old bones.

She sank to the damp ground behind a large gravestone and peered at the settlement house. Lights shone from some of its windows, but still the house looked darker and taller at night, and the bricks appeared black instead of red. Innie rubbed her arms as a cool breeze came up off the water and rattled the tree branches. At her side, she felt Teresa tremble. Nobody said a word.

After a few minutes, the door to the settlement house opened, spreading a pool of warm light on the sidewalk. Innie watched a stream of older girls pour out, humming tunes. But within five minutes or so, the last stragglers had gone, leaving the sidewalks more deserted and silent than before.

The door opened again. A woman's head poked out briefly, then the door slammed shut. "One of the ladies

locking up for the night?" Innie whispered. It was too dark
to tell which one.

"Probably," Matela answered softly. "Now we watch for
something interesting."

"Something scary, you mean," Teresa muttered. She
shivered again.

"Look," Matela said.

The lights on the first floor had gone out. As Innie
watched from the damp burying ground, the second floor
went dark, then the third. At the same time, lights on
the top floor came on, and shadows moved behind the
curtains.

"Do you think whoever comes will wait for the ladies
to go to sleep?" Innie whispered.

"Watch and see." Matela's words made Innie's breath
catch in her throat. Who or what could it be?

Innie stared at the house. Her hands were cold, and
she curled them into fists until her fingernails cut into her
palms. Shadows flitted behind the top-floor curtains again,
and then the lights at the front windows went out. Only a
dim light still showed, perhaps from the bedrooms at the
back of the flat, Innie thought.

A few minutes later, even the dim light had disappeared.
Innie sat up straighter. The house had gone completely
dark. The only light on the street came from distant apartment windows and gaslights half a block away.

Innie started to stand up.

Matela pulled on her arm. "Not yet. Wait. Five minutes. Then we go check all the doors and windows. In front, and back in the alley. If a door or window is unlocked, then maybe the trouble is from a person. But if everything is locked tight, and still something happens, it must be a *mazik* who comes."

Innie didn't know which would be worse. What would they do if they really saw a ghost or a spirit? Or a thief?

With such thoughts rumbling through her mind, Innie couldn't sit another minute. If they didn't go snoop right away, she'd surely run home. She stood, shook the stiffness from her legs, and pointed across the street. "Now, please?"

"Now," Matela agreed.

Tiptoeing single file across the damp grass, they made their way out through the burying-ground gates. On the sidewalk, Innie took one of Teresa's icy hands, and Matela took the other.

"Shh," Matela said. "Careful now."

They crossed the street and climbed the front steps of the settlement house. The door stood in shadows. Innie tried the knob, but it wouldn't turn. "Locked. Let's try the windows," she whispered.

Innie knelt on the sidewalk and checked one of the basement windows, and Teresa checked the other. Both were locked. The first-floor windows—the ones for the shop—were harder to check. They were so high up that Innie could barely touch the bottom of the windowsills.

"I don't weigh so much, Innie," Matela suggested softly. "Let me climb on your shoulders."

Innie knelt to let Matela climb on, then stood, wobbling until she found her balance. She stepped close to one window and felt pressure as Matela tried to force it open.

"Locked. Try the next," came the hoarse whisper.

Innie sidestepped until Matela could reach the second window. Again the pressure, and again nothing happened. "Let me down. They're both shut tight."

"Now what?" Teresa asked.

"We check the back. Through the alley." Matela stepped away from the settlement house, but Teresa shook her head.

"Do we have to? It's so dark back there."

Innie took hold of Teresa's hand. "We've come this far. Please, Teresa. Just a few more minutes."

They crept silently down the block to the alleyway that led to the backyards. Underfoot the cobblestones felt bumpy, and here no gaslights shone. As her eyes grew accustomed to the deeper darkness, Innie made out the shape of the settlement house. She crossed the yard to the back entrance with the other girls right behind her. She tried the door. It would lead to the pottery painting room, but it was locked like the front. Matela climbed to Innie's shoulders and again found the first-floor windows locked tight. There were no basement windows in the back.

"Can we leave now, please?" Teresa tugged hard at Innie's hand.

"Sure. But first let's go back to the front. There's one more thing I need to check," Innie whispered.

When they reached the front of the house again, she stopped and thought. She was sure the kiln room was right under the shop. She closed her eyes to remember on which side of the kiln room she'd seen that strange old door. The right side—she was sure of it—for the windows were on the left. But there was no sign of it from the outside. So that old door stood underground, she realized, right beneath the main front door.

"Can we go home now?" Teresa asked. "I'm so cold."

"Let's watch just a little longer from the burying ground," Innie said. "Now we know all the doors and windows are locked. Let's see if somebody comes and breaks in."

She had barely finished her sentence when a faint glow appeared from one of the basement windows. Teresa yanked on Innie's hand, and the girls ran across the street, back behind the thick stone wall of Copp's Hill.

"No—nobody had time to break in so fast, Innie," Teresa stammered. "So there *is* a ghost in there. It's shining at us."

"A *mazik*," Matela whispered. "We proved it."

"I want to go home right now," Teresa moaned.

Innie frowned. "I don't think it's a ghost or a *mazik*.

Look—the light isn't moving around. I think somebody just turned on the switch. A real person."

"But what person?" Matela asked.

"I think—" Innie said, catching her breath and swallowing hard, "I think we've been here long enough. Let's go home. Right away."

Suddenly, their feet couldn't move fast enough. The girls skimmed down the alleys behind Salem Street all the way to Stillman, where they waited until Matela had sneaked back into her flat. Running now, Innie and Teresa headed back up the hill to their tenement, stopping only when they reached the fire escape.

"Walk me up, Innie. Please."

"Sure."

As quiet as a pair of mice, the cousins slipped up the metal steps. At the top, they both heaved on the window slowly, so it wouldn't squeak. But just as Teresa was easing one leg over the sill, Carmela's voice hissed out at them from the darkness of the room.

"Where have you two been? Innocenza Moretti, what in the name of heaven have you gotten my sister into this time?"

⟨❧

Carmela glared at Innie for the rest of the week. Innie glared right back. The only good thing was that Teresa had somehow convinced her sister not to tell on them, so only Carmela knew how wicked they had been. Innie shuddered to think what Zio Giovanni might do if he knew they'd sneaked out in the dark.

As the cousins talked about the night in the burying ground, Teresa insisted their spying had proved that the troublemaker was a ghost or a *mazik,* and she didn't much care which. She just wanted to stay out of its way.

Innie had her doubts, though, and she kept chewing on them like a piece of hard salami. Something didn't fit. In her mind she went over and over everything she knew. It wasn't until late Saturday afternoon as she and Teresa were walking home from Zio Giovanni's vegetable stall that Innie could fit the pieces together in a way that made sense.

"The thief is no ghost or *mazik,* Teresa," Innie began. "The ladies are right—it's a girl. Probably from one of the library clubs."

"You're crazy, Innie."

Innie kicked a stone on the sidewalk. "Just listen, all right? I've been thinking about this ever since Thursday night. Nothing else makes sense."

Teresa shook her head and walked faster.

Innie pulled Teresa toward a tenement with wide steps and sat down. Teresa stayed standing.

Innie counted out her reasons on her fingers. "Look, first the ladies thought it might be a man stealing, a regular thief, right? But some things didn't stay stolen. Sure, sure, I know the teapot's still missing, but the food got eaten, right there at the settlement house. Remember all the crumbs and walnut shells? And I found the Margaret mug."

"So?" Teresa scowled.

"A real thief would have sold the whole pottery set. Plus there's the missing shawl. What man wants a shawl? And the book that got moved—it was a *girl's* book."

"Don't start with that book again, Innie. It doesn't mean anything. We gotta go home—supper's soon. We got chores."

"Just listen, please. What I think is, some girl is staying at the settlement house at night. When she gets hungry, she takes food—first from the ladies' crate, then from the kitchen. One night she gets cold, so she helps herself to that shawl. And she's there at night with nothing to do, so why not read a book? Every single thing makes sense. Even the lights going on in the basement after the Thursday night club meeting make sense."

"So how does she get in, huh? All the doors and windows were locked. You figure that out, Innie, and maybe I'll believe you. Otherwise, it's a ghost." Teresa folded her arms across her chest.

"I already figured it out," Innie said. "If she goes to one of the clubs, she just stays in the basement after."

"And that Miss Brown doesn't catch her? She's got good eyes and ears—she caught you."

That stopped Innie for a minute. "The girl could hide. In the basement someplace." As she said those words, the last piece of the puzzle slipped into place, and she knew she was right. "Remember that funny old door?"

"What, the little door in the kiln room? It looks like it hasn't been opened in a hundred years, Innie."

"I bet it gets opened every night. I bet there's a little room there, like a root cellar or a closet. The girl hides there until the house gets quiet. Then she comes out and turns on the lights. I'm sure of it."

"A girl wouldn't stay in the basement," Teresa said. "You haven't proved anything."

"But I will," Innie said. "On Monday I'm going to the settlement house. I'm going down in the basement to find out what's behind that door."

"Innocenza Moretti! You'll get yourself in more trouble. Is that what you want?"

"I want to find the thief," Innie said. "And I want you to help."

"Not this time, Innie. Carmela's watching me every minute. You're not getting *me* in trouble again." Teresa spun around and marched up the street.

Innie sat on the steps as if she'd been planted there. "Fine!" she shouted to her cousin's stiff back. "You won't come, I'll go by myself!"

CHAPTER 9
BEHIND THE DOOR

That evening Innie and Nonna hurried to serve the lodgers supper, then went straight upstairs without even washing the dishes. Zia Rachela had invited them up for coffee and special pastry, but she wouldn't tell them the reason. When Innie and Nonna walked into Zia Rachela's kitchen, they found the whole family gathered at the table, where a platter overflowed with napoleons and *cannoli*. Everyone greeted them happily, and Zia Rachela poured cups of coffee.

"What, is this a feast day? Am I so old I have forgotten one of the saints?" Nonna spoke loudly as she surveyed the table.

"A feast day for the Moretti family, Mama," said Zio Giovanni. His smile was so big that his white teeth showed under his bushy black mustache. "We got important news. Sit down and listen good."

Zia Rachela passed the pastries, and even after everybody had helped themselves, there were still sweets left. *Must be some news,* thought Innie.

"I have found a building to buy on Salem Street," Zio Giovanni announced. "The price is good, and I have saved all the money. Tomorrow I go talk to the owner and make an offer on the building. Soon I will have my own grocery store."

Wow, thought Innie. *That is news!*

"Where? How big?" The cousins asked questions faster than Zio Giovanni could answer. Then Nonna's firm voice cut through the others. "This building is brick?"

"*Sì,* Mama. Good, solid brick. Three floors, with an iron fire escape. Let me tell you all about it. On the first floor, a nice big shop at the front. Behind the shop, a storage room, and behind that, three rooms for you and Innocenza. Your own place."

"My own place?"

"A kitchen, two sleeping rooms."

"No more lodgers?"

Innie felt a smile come over her face. No more lodgers! She remembered the kitchen sink downstairs, piled high and waiting for her. No more stacks of dirty dishes to wash. And her own sleeping room.

"You worked hard, Mama. All these years, you cooked and washed for the men and saved up the money. Now you live like a queen, in your own place."

A queen. Innie smiled at the notion. She knew Nonna would be in that shop helping every day.

"What's upstairs, Papà?" Carmela asked.

"Second floor, five rooms. One for Mama and me, one for the boys, one for the girls, a kitchen, and a sitting-in room. Also, on each floor, a sink with running water in the kitchen. A clean white sink. A year or two, we save up, we'll put in a running-water bathtub and one of those flushing toilets."

Innie listened carefully as Zio Giovanni explained his plans. Benito and Mario, her two oldest boy cousins, would take over Zio Giovanni's vegetable stall while her aunt and uncle ran the new grocery. Two businesses instead of just one. And they would rent out the third-floor flat, making more money, until one of her cousins got married and started a family.

Every part of her uncle's plan sounded wonderful to Innie, but her mind kept running back to that clean white sink and a real bathtub. And a flushing toilet—no more nasty privy in the basement. Their house would be like the settlement house. She was so busy imagining how the new flat might look, she missed part of what her uncle was saying.

"So, what do you think? 'Moretti and Sons'? Or just 'Moretti's'? Carmela, my pottery decorator, you will paint the sign, no?"

"Yes, Papà. I'll paint the sign. However you say."

"I say 'Moretti and Sons,'" Antonio announced.

Innie looked at the faces around the table, from Antonio to Teresa. Her gaze stopped at Carmela. "You shouldn't paint *that* sign," Innie said. "'Moretti's,' yes, but not 'Moretti and Sons.'"

"And why not?" Antonio demanded.

Innie frowned at him. "The Moretti family has girls too, that's why not. We'll work in the shop. We'll help a lot."

"Hush, you, Innie," Nonna scolded. "You're just a child, a girl. You must stay out of men's business."

"But this is America," Innie protested.

"Ha, Innocenza," Antonio jeered. "I guess you think Carmela should paint 'Moretti and Daughters,' then? Some sign that would be. The only one like it in all of Boston. Maybe in all of America."

As laughter rose around the table, Innie felt her cheeks grow warm. *I didn't say she should paint "Daughters" on the sign, just "Moretti's." For the whole family. But what do I care? I'm not even a daughter, just a niece.*

Sure, sure, she was a Moretti. She went to Mass with the women of the family and shared in Sunday dinners. And even when she and Teresa got mad at each other like today, they were still best friends.

But no matter what Carmela painted, Innie and Nonna would still live apart, and Teresa's family would still belong to Teresa. Innie would never be anybody's daughter. Painted signs and nice white sinks and running-water bathtubs wouldn't fix that.

❦

Some things you can fix and some you can't, Innie decided later that night. *So I'll fix what I can.*

She spent Sunday laying plans to go back to the settlement house and open that old door. She collected what she needed—her library book, and a screwdriver that her uncle used to pry open vegetable crates. Hoping he wouldn't miss it, she tied it in two handkerchiefs and hid it in her coat pocket. She even got Teresa to promise that she'd tell Nonna their teacher was making Innie stay after school on Monday for missing too much homework. It wasn't true. Innie mostly did her homework, but Nonna would believe the fib.

On Monday after school, Teresa went home alone as planned. Innie headed for the settlement house, sneaking along back alleys and side streets. Once she reached Hull Street, she sorted through her schoolbooks, pulled out her library book, and set it on top of the stack. Now if somebody saw her, she had a reason to be here.

She slipped in the front door with the Monday girls. As they made their way upstairs to the meeting room, she hurried past them through the hall toward the basement door. She thought she heard Miss Guerrier's voice

coming from the second floor. That was good. Now if
she could just sneak by Miss Brown.

Hugging her books to her chest, Innie opened the
basement door and crept downstairs, one step at a time.
At the bottom, she paused to look around. Nobody in
sight. She tiptoed to the kiln room at the front of the
basement and peeked in. It was shadowy and silent. Innie
hurried to the nearest shelf and set down her books.

Reaching into her pocket, she pulled out the screwdriver and untied the handkerchiefs. Her fingers trembled.
It was one thing to brag to Teresa about opening that old
door, but now that she was here alone, it didn't seem so
easy. What if Miss Brown came downstairs and caught
her? What if the thief was hiding on the other side of that
door right now?

Don't be a sissy, she scolded herself. *If you sit around here
and worry, Miss Brown will catch you for sure.*

Innie walked to the old door. She put out her hand
and tried the knob. As before, the knob turned, but the
door stuck fast. She pushed at the top of the little door
and at the bottom. The top moved slightly, so Innie figured that whatever was holding the door shut must be at
the bottom. She knelt and poked Zio Giovanni's screwdriver under the door.

It slid in easily. She ran the blade of the screwdriver
from one side of the door to the other. At the far end,
beneath the knob, she felt something solid. She pulled

out the screwdriver and poked it in again, hard, until she felt the object on the other side give way.

Innie stood and curled her fingers around the knob. "Quiet now," she whispered to the door. "Don't make noise when I open you, or I'm in big trouble."

She turned the doorknob and pushed gingerly. Slowly, the small door opened. A terrible, dank smell hit her nose. Cautiously, Innie peered inside. All she could see was darkness. The only sound she could hear was her own rapid breathing. She ducked her head under the doorway and took a step forward into the darkness. The smell was so bad she could barely breathe.

Innie took another step into the inky blackness. She put out her hand and felt a solid dirt wall on her left—crumbly, cold, and damp. She reached her right hand out to the side and brushed against another dirt wall. She took a step forward, and then another. She didn't bump anything, but the smell got worse, moldy and old and rotting. She reached up. The ceiling of this place, whatever it was, was only inches from her head. She took three more steps and stopped.

Teresa was right, she thought. Nobody had been in this room in a hundred years. Who could hide in this terrible dark hole, with that awful, rotting smell?

Innie turned to leave. Her left foot bumped into something on the floor and it rattled like old bones. Did she dare touch it? She bent and fumbled along the damp, sandy floor.

Near the wall, her hand brushed against something rounded and cold. She moved her fingers along its smooth, circular rim. In the center she found what felt like small wooden balls. Bumpy ones. In the darkness, she picked one up and turned it in her fingers.

Why, those were walnut shells, whole and uncracked nuts. Innie ran her hand around the outside of the container. It felt like a small dish. The Margaret bowl—it had to be! Innie's heart thumped. *I was right after all,* she thought. *The thief has been here.*

Innie reached for the bowl, then pulled her hand back. She wouldn't let that Miss Brown catch her with another piece of missing pottery. But she wanted proof to show Teresa and Matela. She snatched up a walnut and stuck it into her pocket.

On her way out, she stumbled on a small, hard lump. Quickly she picked it up. It felt like a chunk of wood— probably what had been wedged under the door to keep it shut. Innie shoved the wood into her pocket too.

As she shut the door behind her, Innie glanced around the kiln room. It seemed positively brilliant after the foul darkness. She took breath after breath of clean air. Then she tidied herself as best she could, gathered her schoolbooks, and crept up the basement stairs.

When she reached the hall, she spotted Miss Guerrier coming down the stairs from the second floor. The lady saw her too. Innie swallowed hard.

Miss Guerrier walked straight toward her with a serious look in her gray eyes. "Innie? You're here on a Monday? I don't understand."

"I came to return my book," Innie said, hoping she didn't stink from that awful room or have smudges of dirt on her face. She held up the library book. "I wanted to borrow another. I really like that Miss Alcott's stories."

"Very well. Be quick about it. The Monday girls are singing now, but one of my helpers is still in the meeting room putting returned books back on the shelves. She'll help you sign out a new book."

"Yes, Miss. Thank you, Miss." Innie raced upstairs before Miss Guerrier could say another word. On the way back down, she felt like turning cartwheels. She'd done it! She'd opened the old door, found the thief's hiding place, and not gotten caught. She couldn't wait to tell Teresa and Matela. Finding the secret room brought them a step closer to catching the thief, she thought. And the sooner they could do that, the sooner Innie would be out of trouble.

Innie fully intended to go right home. But when she reached the tenement, her feet kept going. *Matela,* she realized. *I've got to tell Matela first. So she can get permission to come snooping tomorrow.* Besides, if Innie could talk Matela into coming, then Teresa would probably come too.

Innie hurried to Stillman Street. During the daytime, Matela's building looked friendlier, just another redbrick tenement with windows along the front and people out on the sidewalk gossiping and bustling here and there. Innie realized that the people were speaking a language she didn't know. And all the women wore scarves over their heads.

She studied a sign in the doorway of Matela's building, but the words were written in curling letters she couldn't read. She tried the door and it was open, so she stepped inside. The hallway was so familiar, Innie felt as if she'd walked into her own tenement. The wooden stairs were steep and narrow, and there appeared to be one flat on each floor. But here, the smell of cabbage filled the hall, instead of the smells of garlic and sausage.

From upstairs she heard the sound of children's voices. That was good, for Innie remembered Matela talking about her little brothers. She started up the steps. In the second-floor hall, Innie noticed some small flat boxes with bits of straw stuck to the sides. They looked like egg boxes. *Matela's egg boxes?* Innie wondered. She knocked at the door. A woman in a long black dress answered. Her hair was tied back in a scarf, and she said something in a language Innie couldn't understand.

"Matela? Matela Rosen, please?"

The woman shook her head and pointed upstairs, holding up three fingers.

"Thank you," Innie said. She climbed another flight of stairs and knocked on the door. A thin woman answered, also wearing a long, dark dress and a scarf.

"Is Matela at home, please?"

The woman studied her for a moment, then called out, "Matela."

When Matela came to the door, she seemed surprised to see Innie there. She was carrying a little boy in her arms. She and her mother spoke for a moment. Innie thought she heard her name mentioned, but she wasn't sure. She didn't like it when people spoke and she couldn't understand. Finally the woman nodded.

"Come in, please," Matela said. "Avrami spills his milk, and I must clean him. Come."

Inside, the Rosens' tenement looked much like the Morettis', crowded with beds and furniture. Innie thought she smelled chicken cooking along with cabbage. In the back room where Matela led her, two slightly older boys sat on the floor between the beds, playing a game with stones. All the boys wore little caps on their heads.

"You come to visit me?" Matela asked.

One of the boys edged toward Innie and peered up at her. "Hello?" he said.

Matela pulled him back. "Please, excuse. This big nosy one, he's Yankel. The middle one is Daniel. Avrami is the baby." She scrubbed at the baby's face with a rag.

Innie wasn't sure what to say. She wrinkled up her nose at the middle brother, Daniel. He laughed. The oldest one stared at her.

"I found something I want to show you at the settlement house," Innie began.

"I can't come out," Matela said. "Mama washes the clothes, and I must keep the boys away from the hot water."

"Could you come with me after school tomorrow?" Innie asked. She lowered her voice to a whisper so Matela's brothers wouldn't hear. "It's that old door. I pried it open. I found the thief's hiding place. It's a hiding place for a real person, not a ghost or *mazik,* and I want to show you." She removed the walnut from her pocket. "Proof. Will your mother let you come out tomorrow?"

"I think so," Matela said, a serious look on her face. "If I do tomorrow's work tonight, she gives some time after school. Yankel can watch the little ones. We meet at the school steps?"

"Sure." Innie paused, then added, "I didn't mean to bother you when you were busy."

"No bother," Matela said quietly. "I tell Mama about you already."

"Tomorrow, then," Innie said as Matela walked her to the door.

On the way home, Innie took a short detour to Saint Leonard's Church. While she walked, she thought about her visit to Matela's. After a few minutes, it hadn't felt so strange, even with Matela's mother speaking a different language. Innie wondered if she might sometime bring Matela home to her house for a visit.

As she ducked into the church through the side door, she remembered Antonio and his threats to tell. Maybe

Zio Giovanni wouldn't like it if Matela visited. Nonna
might not, either.

Innie thought it over. Maybe she'd ask Carmela
what to do. At the settlement house, it didn't seem to
matter whether girls were Italian or Russian, Catholic
or Jewish. Carmela painted pottery with a friend named
Esther Swartzman on one side and a friend named
Angelina Rossetti on the other. Innie and Teresa liked
Matela, so why not invite her to visit?

At the front of the church, Innie knelt before the
Holy Mother's statue, but she didn't pray. Instead she
dropped coins into the box, then looked around to
make sure nobody was watching. With quick fingers,
she reached for three unlit candles and stuck them in
her pocket. Then she slipped back outside and headed
home, still wondering about Matela.

As far as Innie could tell, most of the families in
the North End worked hard, lived in tenements, and
watched out for their families. So what did it matter
if they came from Italy or Russia, went to pray on
Saturday or Sunday?

CHAPTER 10

UNDER COPP'S HILL

 The gray morning dampness had given way to a bright, warm afternoon. Innie and Teresa sat on the school steps soaking up the sunshine as they waited for Matela. As soon as she arrived, they'd head to the settlement house, to the room behind the old door.

Matela had already agreed to Innie's plan, but Teresa was still uncertain. "Oh, Innie, we shouldn't go to Hull Street today," Teresa said. "We'll get in trouble for sure. I just know it."

"What trouble? You brought your library book, didn't you? We're just going so you and Matela can take your books back. That's what I did yesterday. Nobody scolded."

"*And* you broke into that door. Innie, you're bad."

"I'm not!"

"Not what?" Matela asked, coming up behind them. "You don't change your mind, do you?"

"No. Let's go before the Tuesday girls start their club meeting."

Innie and Matela started walking, but Teresa hung back.

Innie turned to her. "You can go home if you want. I'm going to the settlement house."

Matela pulled *The Brown Fairy Book* from the worn cloth bag she had slung over one shoulder. "I also want to borrow a book. So they won't guess."

"Oh, all right," Teresa grumbled.

When they reached the settlement house, younger girls were already arriving for the Tuesday club meeting. Innie, Teresa, and Matela went in with them and hurried upstairs to the book-borrowing table. After choosing a new book and signing it out, Matela winked at Innie and they slipped back into the hallway. Teresa followed.

"Is there a message we have for Carmela?" Innie asked Teresa as they edged toward the stairway. "Just in case."

"In case we get caught, you mean. I can't think of anything. But if we get caught, you can bet Carmela will have plenty to say to *us*."

"So we won't get caught, then. Come on."

The girls crept quickly to the basement. In the corner of the kiln room, Innie tried the old door. It wasn't stuck. "Yesterday, a piece of wood held the door shut, but I took it and threw it away," she explained. "So we can go in now."

"Wait," Matela said. "What if somebody hides there?" She took a step closer and put her ear against the door.

"You hear noises?" Teresa whispered.

"No."

"Let's go in then," Innie said. She turned the knob. As the door opened, a smell of dirt and rotten dampness poured out.

Teresa clutched Innie's elbow, and even Matela said, "Oh, Innie! It stinks, and it's so dark."

"Not for long." Innie reached into her pocket and pulled out a candle and a match. She scratched the match along the rough wood of the door, then touched it to the candle's wick. The flame caught, shedding a soft yellow light.

"Innie, what have you done? Those are church candles!" Teresa said.

"We need to see." Innie reached into her pocket and pulled out two more candles, lit them, and passed them to the other girls.

"But you took them from Saint Leonard's. That's a sin."

"I put money in the box."

"The candles are supposed to stay at church. It *is* a sin, and God will punish you. You and your fire, Innie— it's not right."

"Don't start that again. Not now. We have to see what's in this room."

"The light, it helps," Matela said. She stepped through the doorway. "It is not so scary with a candle. Come, Teresa. We don't want someone to catch us in the basement."

Teresa took one step and coughed.

"Hold the candle up to your face," Innie said. "If you breathe the smoke, you don't smell the bad air so much."

Matela and Teresa stepped farther into the narrow room. Innie joined them and shut the door. Flames from the three candles cast wavering shadows. In the flickering light, the earthen walls seemed to close in on Innie from both sides. The space was so narrow the girls had to walk single file. Ahead of Matela, Innie could see only darkness. The damp, rotting smell surrounded her, and she held her candle closer to her face.

"Keep going, Matela. Let's see how far back it goes," Innie whispered. "Do you see that bowl of walnuts?"

"Here," Matela said. "I see the bowl. Shall we bring it?"

"Let's get it on the way out," Innie said. "I want to keep going."

As they crept on, the walls grew closer together and the ceiling lower. In places, Innie had to duck her head. The smell got worse. There was nothing to see but dim, flickering light, nothing to hear but soft footsteps and her own breathing.

"I think . . ." Matela began in a whisper.

A cobweb brushed across Innie's cheek, and she swatted it away. "What?"

"I think it is not a room you find, Innie."

"What is it?" Teresa's voice sounded high and scared.

"I see no end. We come a long way already. I think it is a tunnel."

A tunnel! Matela had to be right, Innie thought. She wondered where it went, and who had made it, and why. They walked on carefully. Innie held her hand over her nose, but still the foul smell was everywhere. The cold dampness made her shiver.

Ahead, she heard a scraping sound. Then Matela and Teresa stopped walking.

"What?" Innie asked. "What happened?"

"My foot," Matela said. "I step on something hard."

"Innie, let's go back," Teresa said. "Think about where we are right now. We must be walking right under the burying ground."

"Copp's Hill? Maybe. So what?" Even as she said the words, Innie felt a chill creep down the back of her neck.

"So that awful smell could be from—"

"Stop that, Teresa. What did you find, Matela?"

"Something metal—a handle maybe. Partly stuck. I can dig if you will hold my candle." She passed the candle back to Teresa, whose shaking hands made the shadows jump even more.

Innie tried to peer over her cousin's shoulder, but she couldn't see much, only Matela kneeling on the ground pulling on something.

"Ah, I see it. *Oy vay iz mir!*" Matela's voice trembled.

"Oh, Innie! It's a sword," Teresa breathed. "Matela found a sword."

"Is it from the thief?"

"I don't think. Too deep in dirt for that. Come, look."

Innie edged closer, holding her candle high until she could see. The handle and part of the blade showed. If they dug the rest out, the sword would be nearly as big as she was, Innie thought with a shiver.

In the flickering light, she could see rust around the handle and the blade. Why would such a thing be hidden here? "Let's leave this too," she said, swallowing hard. "For later."

As they walked on, the tunnel seemed to wind and twist. Innie sniffed the air. It might have been her imagination, but suddenly it seemed a bit fresher, and saltier.

"Blow out the candles," Matela said from a few feet ahead.

"It will be too dark," Teresa warned.

"I don't think so," Matela said. "Blow them out."

Innie heard the others suck in breath and blow out their candles. She did the same, turning the shadowy tunnel into a black pit. *A black pit with a sword in it,* she thought. Her stomach tightened.

"Look. Up there. I am right." Innie could hear Matela's footsteps, walking faster.

Stuck at the end of the line, Innie couldn't see much, but she followed as quickly as she could. Sure enough, the air smelled cleaner, and salty. Fishy. Ahead, a soft gray light shone. A few steps later, she was standing on a stone pier at the waterfront, looking out on the harbor and

Charlestown beyond. Two ancient wooden posts framed the narrow slit where she stood. There was a rotting fish head by her shoe. Out in the harbor, boats of all sizes bobbed on the tide. If she squinted, Innie could even see men working on some of the boat decks.

"Now we know," Matela said in a strong voice.

Teresa turned to Innie. "I can't believe it. We're outside again. Now we can tell the ladies how the thief is getting in and out. They won't think it's you anymore, Innie."

Innie leaned against one of the wooden posts and shook her head. "Don't be so sure. Yes, we found the way in, but that doesn't prove anything. The ladies could just say *I* was using the tunnel to sneak in." She frowned. "Unless we find the real thief, they'll still blame me."

"I don't like the sound of your voice, Innie Moretti. What are you planning now?"

"She will catch the person," Matela said, grinning. "She will set a trap. Like for a mouse."

"Exactly," Innie agreed. "Here's what we'll do. First, we keep our candles. Next, we come back here to these exact same wood posts . . ." She picked up a loose rock and scratched a line into one of the posts.

Teresa put her hands on her hips. "You're crazy, Innie. I'm not going back in that tunnel." She turned and pointed toward the burying ground. "It goes right under the graves. It smells like dead people in there. Some people call it *Corpse* Hill, you know."

"Coward."

Teresa's face darkened. "You're always getting us in trouble. Well, this time it's too much. I quit." Teresa flung her candle on the ground.

"Fine. Just go home then. Coward!" Innie picked up Teresa's candle and shoved it in her pocket.

"Troublemaker!" Teresa spun and ran along the harbor.

Innie stood and watched until her cousin had run out of sight.

Matela cleared her throat. "That is not so nice."

"*La vità è così,*" Innie replied.

"But you and Teresa. You are like sisters. Now you are like enemies. Not good."

"Sisters fight too," Innie said. "Besides, it's better this way. Teresa can't keep secrets. So if she doesn't know when we come back to find the thief, she can't tell anyone." She straightened her shoulders. "We're better off without her."

"Innie, you do not mean this. I see you together. You laugh, you whisper. I wish for myself such a cousin. You hurt Teresa."

Matela's words carried the sting of truth. Innie pushed it away. "That's because I'm a bad person. Just ask anyone. I'm always making trouble."

Matela took Innie's hand. "And why is that? Why make trouble? My papa says trouble comes plenty without we go look for it."

"Maybe I like looking for it." Innie pulled her hand

from Matela's. She bent and picked up a pebble, then tossed it in the water.

Matela stood beside her. "I too am a coward in that tunnel," she said in a quiet voice. "That sword. It makes me remember . . ."

"What?"

"The soldiers. They ride those big black horses and wave swords and shout . . ."

"Back in Russia?"

"Yes. The swords and the fires, I can't forget. Sometimes at night . . ." Matela turned her face away.

Innie reached out and touched her arm. "Fire—that's . . . that's part of the reason for me," Innie began. Her throat felt so tight it was hard to get the words out. She'd never talked about this before.

"If you tell, I can listen. I do not repeat secrets," Matela said softly.

Innie looked out on the choppy water where a lone white seagull bobbed. She turned to her friend. "This is a long story, Matela. It starts back in Italy, before the fire, before I was even born."

Innie paced along the stones of the pier as she told Matela the story Nonna had whispered to her so many times. About how Innie's mama had prayed and prayed for a child, but always the babies were born too early and died. How once Mama came to America, her luck changed and she had a baby who lived.

Matela's eyes went soft. "You?"

"Me. Mama was so happy, and so grateful to God. On the day I was taken to church to be baptized, she lit candles to the Holy Mother and promised my life to her."

"I don't understand. We Jews don't have this."

"Nonna says Mama promised me to the Holy Mother and—and to the Sisters. You know, the nuns. They wear long black dresses, and veils on their heads. They never get married, and they pray all the time."

Matela nodded. "I see those ladies. But what does this mean? Promise you to the Sisters?"

"When I grow up, I have to be a nun. One of those Sisters. I'll have to wear a long ugly dress and chop off my hair and pray all the time."

Innie looked away from Matela. The hardest part was still coming. She scuffed the toe of her shoe against the stone pier and spoke fast, to get it over with.

"Anyway, when I was two, I woke up early one morning, fussing and crying. Nonna took me outside to walk by the harbor so Mama and Papà could sleep. When we got back, the tenement was burning. Mama and Papà died."

An arm came around Innie's shoulder. "Oh, Innie. This is so sad. And you are just a baby then."

Innie swallowed and went on. "After the fire, Nonna decided that the Holy Mother had been the one to make me wake up and cry on that day. The crying saved her life and mine. So she took me to church and again, she promised me to the Sisters. My life got promised away twice." Now she'd said it all. Innie was afraid to turn and see what Matela thought.

"Can somebody promise you like that?" Matela asked. She scowled and shook her head. "In Russia, parents and matchmakers, they try to marry you off. But even there, if the girl says no, there is no wedding."

"So?"

"This is America. A girl can choose her life here, can't she?"

"You don't understand—you're not Catholic." Innie's voice got small. "The best I can do is act so bad that the Sisters won't want me." It wasn't that Innie woke up every morning and thought about what mischief she could get into; she just didn't make the effort to be good. If naughtiness came upon her, she'd shrug and say *Sure, why not, who cares?* But how could she explain that to Matela?

"So you make trouble. Oh, Innie . . ." Matela giggled. "Now I understand. I don't mean to laugh, but it is funny. You are so *good* at being *bad*."

This was a mistake, Innie thought. *I never should have told.* She turned away. "Everybody gets to be good at something, I guess."

Matela shook her shoulder with a firm hand. "No, no. We must ask somebody. About this promising. The Sisters? Surely they know."

"I can't ask. It would get back to my family. At
Saint Leonard's, everybody knows each other and every-
body else's business. Zia Rachela says it's like a little
Italian village."

"My *shul* is like that too," Matela said. "But Boston's
big. Go to another church. Not in the North End." She
pointed across the harbor. "Over there. I see steeples."

Innie shrugged. "Sure, they have Catholic churches in
Charlestown. Lots of Irish people live there. But I can't . . ."

"Now who is the coward? Charlestown. I'll . . . I'll go
with you."

Innie spoke gently. "No, Matela. A church would be
too hard. All those crosses."

Matela's chin came up and her face took on a stubborn
look. "Those crosses are in the old country. A long time
ago. Now we have a new country. We try new things."

"But you . . ."

"I and you, both, new girls in a new place. Not stuck
with the old. No more *azoy gayt es,* no more give in to the
old times. No more *vita* . . ."

"No more *la vita è così?*"

"Right. Things only go bad if we let them. And we
don't let them. We find the tunnel, which is deep in the
ground. So how hard is it to find an answer? These Sisters
you talk of, they don't carry swords, do they?"

CHAPTER **11**

NO LONGER WELCOME

Innie couldn't sleep that night. First thing next morning, she patched up her argument with Teresa. But still, during school she had trouble concentrating, and her teachers scolded. By afternoon, she couldn't wait to get to the settlement house, where it was calm and clean, and where people were kind.

Not long after Innie, Teresa, and Matela arrived, Miss Guerrier called the Wednesday afternoon girls into a circle. She sat with *The Prince and the Pauper* on her lap, but she didn't open the book. She looked at each girl in turn.

"Before I begin to read today, I have some serious news to share," she said. "Once again, a thief has come to the settlement house."

Innie wasn't imagining it—Miss Guerrier's eyes were fixed on her face. Matela took her hand and squeezed it gently, but still, Innie's chest tightened and it was suddenly hard to breathe.

"Money was stolen from the pottery shop downstairs," the woman continued. "Miss Brown and I will deal most severely with the culprits when we discover them."

Innie's heart thudded. Did those Yankee ladies somehow know that Innie, Matela, and Teresa had been in the settlement house yesterday? Had somebody seen them? Innie didn't dare look at Matela or Teresa. Instead she stared straight ahead and squeezed Matela's hand, hard.

Miss Guerrier opened the book and began to read, but for once in Innie's life, the words from a book gave her no comfort. She barely heard them. All she could hear were the words Miss Guerrier had said earlier, pounding in her head like drums. *We will deal most severely with the culprits when we discover them.*

Innie's voice sounded sour in her ears during the singing. She couldn't seem to breathe right or remember the words to the songs. Her feet forgot the steps of the dances, and she stumbled twice. Only Matela's hand kept her from disgracing herself.

When club time was over and the Wednesday girls hurried to the hall for coats and sweaters, Miss Guerrier stopped Innie, Teresa, and Matela. "Please come into the music room for a moment," she told them.

They followed her in, and she shut the door. "Now, do you know anything about our most recent troubles?"

Innie couldn't think of a thing to say.

"The money?" Matela asked.

"You said somebody took it," Teresa added.

Innie curled her hands into fists. She couldn't let her cousin keep talking. Even if Teresa didn't mean to say anything about their snooping, she'd let something slip. Innie spoke fast. "When did you find the money gone? Today was the first we heard of anything else missing."

"The thief must have come sometime between Monday afternoon and Tuesday evening. You, Innie, were here on Monday. I saw you."

Miss Guerrier's eyes bored into Innie's. It felt as if the woman could see right into her thoughts.

"Until the thief is caught, we are suspending house time for all the girls. You will not come to work tomorrow." Miss Guerrier let out a sigh. "This is such a disappointment to Miss Brown and me. So much good can come from our activities at the settlement house. It would be a shame if one or two persons ruined it for all."

"Yes, ma'am," Innie whispered.

When Matela spoke, Innie felt as if she'd been rescued. "Yes, ma'am, no work tomorrow. We come again to club next Wednesday, then?"

"Indeed. You and Teresa may come." Miss Guerrier's voice was stern, and her face looked sharp and pointy.

"What about me?" Innie asked softly. "Can't I come?"

"Wait here." She turned and strode toward the kitchen. When she returned, she was holding something in her right hand.

Innie turned cold when she saw Zio Giovanni's screwdriver. *How could I have been so dumb?* Innie asked herself. *How could I forget such a thing?*

"Have you seen this before, Innie? You'll notice the initials *GM* scratched into the wooden handle. Could the *M* stand for *Moretti?*" Miss Guerrier held the handle right under Innie's nose.

Innie stared at Zio Giovanni's initials. Her voice failed her; she could only nod. Her cheeks burned and her eyes filled.

"Just as I thought. The cash box was pried open, and we found this screwdriver on the floor of the shop."

No, Innie thought. *I left it in the basement, in the kiln room. By the old door.*

"You may confess if you wish. Until such time as we have reason to believe otherwise, Miss Brown and I consider you the thief. You are no longer welcome here, Innie. I'm sorry." Miss Guerrier turned coldly and left the room.

Innie ran for the hall. She grabbed her coat, ran downstairs, and stumbled out the front door.

❧

"How can they think such a thing?" Matela asked when she and Teresa caught up to Innie on the sidewalk. "You are no thief. You are trying to help."

"Oh, Innie, I know you're not the thief," Teresa said. "But—but what if Carmela loses her job because of this? I need to go home and tell Mama." She hurried around a couple of schoolboys playing on the sidewalk.

Misery and more misery, Innie thought. Everything she did went wrong. "Wait, Teresa, don't tell yet, please. Let me think what to do."

"Do? Do? Nothing is what we can do. They won't even let us come for house time. Oh, Carmela will be so mad."

"We will go back to the tunnel and find the real thief," Matela said quietly.

"We could at least tell the ladies about the tunnel," Teresa said. She stopped walking and leaned against a lamppost.

Innie frowned. "That's not enough to prove I didn't take the money. Or the silver teapot. We have to go back inside the tunnel and trap the thief."

"Yes. In the basement," Matela said. "But not tomorrow. Tomorrow they watch everything—very careful. And the day after, that is Friday, when *Shabbos* begins. From sunset Friday until sunset Saturday, I cannot come out. Can you come out on Saturday night?"

"We can't," Teresa said. "Carmela, she's a Saturday evening girl. She has her club meeting at the settlement house until nine o'clock. She'll come home at nine-thirty and find me gone. So I can't sneak out. Not on Saturday."

Innie could tell that Teresa was glad for an excuse to

say no. But Innie didn't want to waste even one extra day. "What time does Carmela go to sleep on Saturday nights?"

"Innie, you can't mean—"

"What time?" Innie repeated. "Ten o'clock? Ten-thirty?"

"Ten-thirty, maybe. But, Innie—"

"So we leave the house when? Eleven? Maybe eleven-thirty, just to be safe?"

"Safe?" Teresa sputtered. "Innie, you're crazy. Don't you listen to Papà? No girl is safe out alone at night. And the later it gets, the more dangerous it is."

"But we will be three," Matela said. "We are small and quick, and no one will see us."

"Let's plan to meet at Copp's Hill again," Innie said. "At midnight, just to make sure Carmela's asleep."

"Midnight? In a burying ground? Now I know you're crazy." Teresa's cheeks were flushed.

"Nine o'clock or twelve o'clock—if we get caught, what difference does it make? If you don't come, Matela and I will go without you."

Teresa just glared at her, then stomped off up the street.

"Innie," Matela said. "Teresa or not, we will catch the thief soon."

"I guess so." Innie shook her head. "But I hate to waste tomorrow doing nothing."

Matela stepped close to Innie and spoke softly. "We do not waste tomorrow. Mama thinks I have house time, so I don't have to help at home."

"What are you getting at?"

"Charlestown." Matela pointed across the harbor where a tall church steeple stretched toward the sky. "That mystery we solve tomorrow."

Innie looked over the water. Had she heard right? Did Matela really want to go ask about all that promising?

She turned to see Matela's dark eyes staring at her solemnly, and they made Innie feel ashamed. If Matela was brave enough to visit a church, the least Innie could do was dig up the courage to ask questions and wait for the answers. After that, meeting at midnight in a burying ground shouldn't be hard at all.

⚬❦⚬

After school the next day, Innie picked another fight with her cousin. Teresa marched home alone, and Innie hurried to the Charlestown bridge to meet Matela.

Matela was waiting there for her. "What? No Teresa?"

"I couldn't tell her about this. She'd spill it to the family. Bad enough they'll find out about the settlement house trouble. I don't want Carmela to know about the promising. And those boys, never!"

"All right. You ready?"

"I guess."

Matela didn't have much to say as they crossed the bridge into Charlestown and climbed the hill toward the tallest church steeple they could see. Innie tried not to think about the questions she would ask the Sisters. With the sun warming her shoulders, she concentrated on walking and breathing in the spring air, scented with flowers and salt and the sea. Everywhere she looked, green leaves were bursting, painting the city with life again after the long, chill winter. It might have been a day like this when the fire happened, she thought. Only a little later. June seventh, that was the day her parents had died.

To reach the church, the girls had to climb to the top of a steep hill. Soon they stood on the steps at the side doorway of Saint Francis' Church.

Innie kept walking, but Matela didn't. Innie stopped and turned around.

Matela's face had gone even paler than usual. "Innie, I can't come in. I thought I could help you, but it's too hard."

"It's all right. Really. I'll go ask my questions, and you can wait outside."

Matela didn't smile. She wouldn't look Innie in the eye.

"I mean it, Matela. You don't have to come along." Innie reached into her pocket for a handkerchief to cover her head. She turned back toward the church and practically crashed into a black-robed priest. "Sorry, Father. I was clumsy."

He smiled. "I was also clumsy. I'm sorry."

Innie studied the priest. He had a round face with red cheeks, and graying hair. He'd probably know the answers to her questions, she thought. In his black cassock, he looked strict, more serious than the brown-robed Franciscan fathers at Saint Leonard's. But those priests knew the Morettis, and this one was a stranger. Innie figured she could talk to him. She opened her mouth to speak, but her throat froze.

"We come across the bridge for a question," Matela began, her voice shaking.

She's never talked to a priest in her life, Innie thought. *These are my questions. I can't make her do the asking. It isn't fair.*

"Father, I came to ask about being a Sister."

His eyebrows went up in surprise. "A nun? Well, you seem a bit young to profess a vocation. Tell me how you've come to such a decision."

"I don't. I mean, I didn't. I . . ."

"Come, let's sit down. We will speak more easily." He sat on a stone step. Innie and Matela did the same.

"Now, about you being a Sister?"

Bit by bit, Innie explained about her mother's promising, then Nonna's.

"I see. So your mother named you Innocenza for purity, and Maria, to honor the Holy Mother. Innocenza Maria. A fine name for a fine girl," the priest said. "You're Italian, aren't you? From the North End?"

"Yes, Father. Salem Street."

"As I said, a fine girl. Not every girl would cross the bridge into Charlestown to get her questions answered."

"My friend came too. She helped."

"And you are . . . ?" he asked Matela with a kind smile.

"Matela Rosen. I am Jewish and from Russia."

The priest's eyebrows went up again, and he paused for a moment. "Another fine girl. And a good friend, to help."

He turned back to Innie. "From what you've told me, this promising has weighed heavily on you, Innocenza. Surely your mother and grandmother had reason to be grateful, to ask God's blessings on you and to give thanks for you." He smiled gently at her. "It is a good thing to consecrate a child to God."

Innie's heart thudded in her chest. She wanted to plug up her ears, for it sounded as if the priest was about to agree that her future was already decided.

"But I think that perhaps your family used the wrong words when they prayed about you. No one can *promise* another's life," he said firmly. "Becoming a nun is a holy and serious choice, one made by a grown person after much prayer and soul-searching."

Was he saying that she might be free after all? Innie needed to make sure. "I've heard about girls left on convent steps, given to the Sisters . . ."

"Yes. Sometimes our Sisters of Mercy tend to orphans or lost children. But they don't try to turn them into nuns and priests, just good Catholics. And that is what I pray you will become, Innocenza. A good Catholic girl who will grow into a good Catholic woman. Whether or not your heart leads you to a vocation, well, that's in God's hands."

Suddenly Innie's shoulders felt so light, she wondered if she might float right up to where the spire of Saint Francis' met the sky. "Thank you, Father."

The priest stood and put his hands out. "Bless you. Bless you both. Now go on home. Your families will be looking for you." He made his way down the steps and crossed the street.

Innie stood and took a deep breath of the warm, fragrant air.

Matela flung an arm around her and spun her in a circle. "What did I tell you? In America, you choose for yourself."

As they walked to the corner, Innie felt like dancing. "Thank you, Matela. I never could have come here without you."

"It's all right. I'm sorry I cannot go inside."

"You made me come here. That was plenty."

Matela nodded. "You know, that Father, he isn't so bad. For the first time ever, somebody with a cross says a blessing on me, not a curse."

"That's good, then," Innie said.

"One more thing," Matela began. "Can I . . . can a Jewish person pray next to a Catholic church? Is it allowed?"

"I think so. Sure, why not? Did you pray back there on the steps?" *What a brave thing to do,* Innie thought.

Matela nodded. "I pray for two things. I pray for us to find the thief. Saturday night, like we plan—so you can come back to the library club. Until you go back, I too will not go, for you are my friend."

Innie didn't know what to say. Her throat went dry.

Matela grinned at her. "Also, I pray to say thank you. Now you are not promised anymore. So you can be good sometimes. No more big fights with Teresa, yes?"

"Oh, Matela!" Innie laughed and threw an arm around Matela's shoulder.

But as they walked down the streets of Charlestown toward the bridge and home, Innie couldn't help but wonder. Now that she knew she didn't have to become a Sister, did she have to do what Matela said? Being bad was easy. But being good would take a lot of work.

CHAPTER 12
AN AMERICAN PARTNER

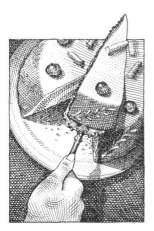

When Innie arrived home, she found Zia Rachela sitting on the tenement steps waiting for her, with a stern look on her face.

"Where have you been, Innocenza?"

"I . . ."

"You turn my household upside down, and then you disappear. First you hurt my Teresa's feelings, so she comes home crying and upsets her sister, who is missing work to study for the citizen hearing on Friday. Then Carmela bangs books and stamps her feet. Boom. She's like a firecracker, that one. So now you must tell me where you go and why."

Innie twisted the handkerchief in her coat pocket. She looked around the busy sidewalk. "Out here? With all these people around?"

"All right, come up to the kitchen. But talk quiet. Carmela is in the back room studying again, and Teresa rests on my bed."

As she climbed to the second floor behind her aunt, Innie was tempted to make up a big whopper of a story, but she couldn't. Not today. Today, she wanted to be good. She took a chair at the kitchen table and breathed in the spicy smells of supper cooking.

"So?"

"I went to church, Zia Rachela. I needed to go."

"What? Church? You went to Saint Leonard's to ask forgiveness for the fight with your cousin? That's fast."

"No. Not for forgiveness, and not to Saint Leonard's either. Oh, Zia Rachela!" It was just too much. Innie felt her eyes fill, and she couldn't stop the tears from pouring out. She put her head down on the table.

She felt her aunt's hand rubbing her back gently. After a moment she sat up. "I *did* fight with Teresa, and I'm sorry. I picked the fight on purpose. I didn't want her to come with me."

"Why not?"

"I went over to Saint Francis' Church, in Charlestown, where they wouldn't know me. I had questions, and if I asked at Saint Leonard's, everybody would find out. They'd laugh."

"This sounds important."

"Just to me," Innie whispered. Then she stared at the rough tabletop and told her aunt about the promising, and what the priest had said. As Innie talked, Zia Rachela slid her chair closer and took hold of Innie's hand.

"All this time, you worry about becoming a Sister?"

"Yes."

"You don't ask anybody?"

"Who could I ask? Nonna's the one who promised me away. I know what she wants."

"Nonna, your grandmother . . . she scares you sometimes?"

Innie nodded. "Sometimes."

"That I understand. She scares me sometimes too. So strong. So sure."

Innie turned and studied her aunt's face. The kindness in her eyes made Innie sorry she'd caused trouble today.

"You could ask me your questions, *bambina*. I would find you answers. Good answers."

Innie shrugged. "You're busy. You have your own family."

"And you are *not* my family? Innocenza Maria Moretti! You are not the child of my body, no. But *bella mia*—you are the child of my heart. My own girls and boys, I love them, yes. Each one is beautiful to me. But you—with your brave heart and all alone in the world—you I love in a special way."

Zia Rachela's arms came around Innie and held her tight. Innie didn't even try to hold her tears inside. She just let go and let herself be surrounded by those warm, loving arms.

A few minutes later, after the crying stopped, Innie pulled away. "I need to talk to Teresa. To explain."

"Yes, you do. But you don't have to tell your secrets if you don't want. Just say you needed to speak to the priest about some serious matters, and you didn't know how to explain. She will understand. My Teresa, she has a good heart."

Yes, she does, Innie thought. She smiled at her aunt. *Just like you.*

⁌

Friday, Innie felt tired, but a good kind of tired. Teresa had forgiven her and not asked nosy questions. Even better, she'd agreed to join Innie and Matela in the search for the thief.

In school, Innie worked her arithmetic carefully and rechecked each problem. One good thing at a time, she decided. That was hard enough. After school, she and Teresa hurried home to find out how Carmela's citizen hearing had gone. Zia Rachela was smiling, and she put them to work right away in the kitchen.

That evening, the Morettis celebrated. There was so much food, Innie thought, it would take a week to eat it all. Zio Giovanni poured glasses of sweet vermouth for a toast.

Buona fortuna! Molta felicità! Per cent'anni! Happiness for a hundred years.

Wow! A hundred years. Innie couldn't imagine such

a long time. She and Teresa got half-glasses of vermouth, which they raised to honor Carmela. She looked even more beautiful than usual today, wearing her blue suit with a gardenia in her lapel. She looked as stylish as those Yankee ladies, Innie decided. And why not, now that she was American too?

"Thank you, thank you." Carmela smiled at everybody, even Innie. *She won't be smiling when she hears they kicked me out of the settlement house,* Innie thought. *But maybe she won't have to know. If we catch the thief tomorrow night . . .*

"So the questions from the judge, are they hard?" Zio Giovanni asked as they began their soup. "You studied those books every night."

"Yeah," Antonio said. "You gonna stop stomping around the house and slamming doors now, Miss American Citizen?"

Carmela made a face at him. "We got three American citizens here now." She waved three fingers at him. "All girls. When are you boys gonna catch up? I'll give you lessons so you can be smart like us." Carmela took Teresa's and Innie's hands in hers and squeezed.

"Sure, sure."

Innie grinned. The laughter around the table warmed her as much as the rich chicken soup did, and she liked having Carmela brag about her for once. "Good times for the Moretti family," she said. "Uncle finds a building and Carmela makes a citizen."

The table went silent. Innie looked around. "What?" she asked. "What did I say wrong?"

Zio Giovanni cleared his throat. "The news on my building, it isn't so good."

"What happened? Did somebody else buy it?"

"No, it's not that. It's all the papers." He stood and reached for a thick stack of papers from a shelf by the window. Zia Rachela took away the soup plates and brought pasta with meat sauce. Zio Giovanni tossed the papers into the middle of the table.

"Papers, papers," her uncle complained. "In America a man can choke on papers."

Zia Rachela explained. "All those pages. Laws about buying property. All in English. Your uncle and me, we don't read English so good."

Zio Giovanni interrupted. "How can I sign papers I don't understand? I show the papers to Benito, to Mario. But it's no good. So many long, complicated words, even my sons get mixed up. At the Italian Benevolent Society, the man says hire a Yankee lawyer, but I say no. I don't trust my business to some stranger."

Innie couldn't believe her ears. Her dreams of a fancy house with a big white bathtub were stuck in a pile of papers. "There must be something we can do."

"Oh, yeah," Antonio interrupted. "Innie the big shot. *She's* gonna read all those hundred-dollar words. She's gonna fix Papà's business."

Innie sat up straighter and looked her uncle right in the eye. "I can't fix your business. But somebody can." She turned and pointed. "Carmela. She read all those books for her citizen hearing. And I saw the pages—full of hundred-dollar words. Carmela could read your papers."

The table exploded in shouts. "What, a girl?" "Stupid!"

Nonna scowled at Innie. "You, hush. Little girls have no place in such talk."

"That's not true, Nonna," Carmela said. She threw an arm around Innie. "She's got a good idea. Papà, could I help? Anything I can't understand, I can look up. I did plenty of that for the hearing."

Zia Rachela smiled. "Giovanni, how about it? Will you let Carmela help? She's American now, remember."

"So what, now I got an American partner?" He frowned and pointed his finger at Carmela. "You read my papers, maybe. But you don't run the business."

"I don't want to, Papà. I like painting pottery."

"*You* run the business, Giovanni," Zia Rachela said. "But when the business and the family grow so big we need to buy the building next door to that shop, I'm gonna be the next American partner. Starting tomorrow, Carmela's gonna teach me to read English. If you're smart, Giovanni, you'll study too."

"What, you want us all to be American, Mama?" Benito asked.

"We're here, aren't we? So, yes, we'll be an American family."

"Not me," Nonna said in a firm voice. "I'm born Italian and I'll die Italian."

Zia Rachela smiled gently. "Yes, Mama. I understand. So we'll be what then? An Italian family with an American business? We'll make lots of American money. Is that good enough?"

"Good enough," Nonna agreed.

Then Zia Rachela brought out a fancy cake decorated with fruit and nuts, and she gave everyone double helpings of the sweet *cassata*.

Afterward, as the women and girls cleaned the kitchen, Zia Rachela took Innie aside. "You had a good idea, *bambina*. Your uncle may not come out and say the words, but I know he's grateful. He's bragged to all his friends about this building of his, and if he doesn't buy it, he'll lose face. *Grazie*."

"All this American talk, though, it upsets Nonna," Innie said.

Zia Rachela nodded. "Most of her life, she lived in Italy, and her memories are there. Change is a struggle. But we'll be kind to her. Besides, the North End is full of old people from the old country. She has many friends to remember the old days with."

"How about you, Zia Rachela? Will it be hard for you?"

"The studying, sure. But I'm ready. Too long, I've felt

like some bridge. Nonna in the old country, my children in the new, me in the middle, not belonging to either place. So now it's decided. I'm going to belong to America."

"I'll help you study," Innie promised. "I'll bring home books, lots of books, and read out loud to you."

Then Innie remembered—she couldn't borrow those books unless the ladies let her back into the library club. She *had* to find the thief to prove her innocence. If she didn't, she couldn't help her aunt.

Tonight had been a celebration, but now Innie was feeling sour. Oh, why did everything have to be so complicated, she wondered. Why couldn't life be as sweet as Zia Rachela's fruit-covered *cassata*?

CHAPTER 13
MIDNIGHT

The streets were nearly deserted on Saturday night as Innie and Teresa crept up the sidewalk toward the Old North Church.

As they neared the church, the steeple clock slowly began to chime the hour. *Bong. Bong. Bong.* Innie and Teresa hurried past the church and the wall of the burying ground. At the stroke of midnight, they stood at the tall iron gates and peered in. After the tolling of the bell, a hush fell on the graveyard. The skin on Innie's arms tingled.

"Matela? Matela, are you here?"

No answer.

"Innie, should we go home? It's so dark and so cold."

Innie breathed in the chill salt air and wrestled with her conscience. Here she was trying to be good, and at the very same time starting another something *bad*. But the sooner they caught the thief, the sooner she could be all-the-time good. What was a night's worth of mischief compared to that?

"Button your coat, Teresa. Feel how quiet the night is. We've never been out so late except for Christmas Eve."

Innie felt Teresa shiver beside her.

"Shh. Footsteps." Innie ducked inside the gates of the burying ground, pulling Teresa along. They peered out, watching the sidewalk. Across the street, the settlement house looked quiet and dark except for a faint glow from the basement windows. The light seemed dimmer than before, so pale that if a person weren't looking for it, she might not notice. But Innie was looking. The thief was inside.

"Someone's coming," Teresa whispered. "Looks like Matela."

Innie and Teresa crept out to the sidewalk, and Matela rushed toward them. "Good. You come already. No waiting."

"The thief's already there. Look, lights." Innie pointed to the basement windows. Matela nodded.

As silent as shadows, the three girls made their way across the burying ground toward the harbor, keeping to the grass so their shoes wouldn't make noise on the path. They crested the hill and carefully climbed down the other side and over the stone wall. Edging along the damp, slippery stones of the pier, they soon saw the pair of rotting wood posts that marked the tunnel entrance.

"Ready?" Innie scratched one of Nonna's kitchen matches on the stone wall. Its flare cast a glimmer on the dark, lapping water. Innie lit her candle and held it out so the others could light theirs. Then they stepped between the posts into the tunnel.

As before, Matela led the search party, with Teresa safely in the middle and Innie at the end. Inside the tunnel, it shouldn't have made a difference that night had come, but somehow it did. Noises seemed to echo; their footsteps sounded like giants' instead of girls'. And the rotting smell grew worse the farther into the tunnel they crept.

Innie had to force herself to keep going, to keep walking into the darkness. They'd gone perhaps a third of the way when she had to slow down and duck to keep from bumping her head on a low part of the dirt ceiling. She thought she heard a faint sound, like a dropped stone, somewhere behind her. "Shh," she warned the others. "Walk quieter."

She turned and held up her candle, but saw nothing in the shadowy darkness. She tried to shake off her unease and hurry along.

At a curve in the tunnel, Innie stood silent for a moment. They had to be under the burying ground now. Innie felt her heart beat faster just thinking about it. But she didn't dare lose courage. She kept walking, staying close to Teresa. Nobody spoke.

When the tunnel straightened again, Innie put her hand out to touch Teresa's arm. They had to be under the street now, nearing the house. If the tunnel door was open, their lights would soon show. They took several more steps, then Matela stopped.

"Now," Matela whispered.

Innie blew out her candle. Matela did the same and then Teresa. They stood in blackness, trying to let their eyes adjust. Innie's heartbeat drummed in her ears. She inched forward, feeling along the damp dirt wall with her left hand. She felt rather than heard Matela stop. Crowding close to the others, she reached out, and her fingers brushed lightly against wood. The old door.

Matela's counting was more a breath than a whisper— "One, two, three . . ." She twisted the knob and pulled. The door swung open.

The kiln room stood in darkness. The only light came from the basement hallway. Innie blinked. At first she saw nothing unusual. Then, as she looked more closely, she spotted a dark shape on the floor next to the kiln. Could it be the thief?

The three girls tiptoed forward until they stood in a circle around a sleeping form. Innie's breath whooshed out of her chest. It was a girl after all. And she had to be the thief because she was wrapped up in a nice-looking shawl, while the rest of her clothes were tattered and filthy. Her light brown hair hadn't been brushed in a long time, and what Innie could see of her face was smudged.

"What do we do now?" Teresa was staring so hard at the girl, it made Innie want to step back.

"We wake her up maybe?" Matela whispered.

"I guess so." Innie made no move toward the sleeping girl. It didn't seem right, somehow, even if she was the thief, to sneak up on her while she was sleeping.

Matela reached out and touched the girl's shoulder, shaking it gently. "Hello, you."

The girl jumped and sat up right away. "What? Who? Oh dear heavens!" She pulled the shawl tighter around her shoulders.

Matela stepped toward the doorway and switched on the electric bulb. With better light, Innie studied the girl's face—thin, with a pointed chin, and hair more red than brown.

"Who—who are you?" The girl's voice was high and soft, and scared.

Well, she ought to be scared, Innie decided. *She's a thief.* She took a step forward. "I'm Innie Moretti. Who are you?"

"Why do you come here?" Matela asked sternly.

The girl by the kiln wouldn't look at them. She hid her face in her hands, and Innie could see her shoulders shaking. Judging by the girl's size, Innie guessed she wasn't much older than they were.

"Please don't cry. Maybe we can help." Teresa knelt next to the strange girl.

"Who are you?" Innie repeated. "What's your name?"

The girl sniffed. "I'm Katie—Kathleen Mulrooney."

"You've been staying here, haven't you? Taking things?"

The girl looked at them for a long moment. "Aye, I had no place else to go." She looked down. "I only took what I needed to live—a bit of food, a couple of dishes. A . . . a few coins. I mean to pay it all back soon, truly I do."

"Why do you come here?" Matela asked. "How do you find this tunnel?"

"Please tell us, Katie," Teresa added.

Innie didn't understand how Teresa could be so polite to this thief who had caused them so much trouble. But it seemed to work. Katie's shoulders relaxed a bit.

"It's a long story, it is," she said softly. "I came to America three months past. I had a fine job too, didn't I? Maid in a fancy house, and I was earning good wages. Good enough so I'd put some by to bring me sisters and me mum to America one day. Then that terrible fire started . . ."

Innie stiffened. "The Chelsea fire?" For a moment, she saw again the smoke billowing over the harbor, heard the booming explosions.

Katie nodded.

"What happened?" Teresa asked softly.

"The grand house burned, didn't it? Right down to the stones. Everybody ran off with nothing but the clothes on their backs. Thousands of people there were, all over Chelsea, running from the fire. I looked and

looked, but I couldn't find the missus or the mister anywhere. I searched for two days and two nights. Finally,
I came here."

"How do you know about the tunnel?" Matela asked.

"Ah, our cook, she was one for the stories. She liked
to scare us is what, always talking about dark places and
spiderwebs. When she was a child, she lived here, in the
North End. She and her friends used to play in the tunnel,
she said. Liked to hide from folks. Once on my half day,
I persuaded her to show me."

Teresa leaned closer. "So when the fire burned down
the house . . ."

"I came to the tunnel, aye. I knew I'd be dry at least.
And then I found that the tunnel led here, to this fancy
cooker." She reached out and touched the brick kiln lightly.
"When it's turned on, it's warmer than the outside. So
sure, I stayed."

"But you must not take things here," Matela added.
"Other people, they get in trouble." She glanced at Innie.

Katie turned to Innie, then looked down. "I didn't
mean to get anyone in trouble. But I was so cold, and so
hungry. I've done wrong, I know, but I am sorry . . ."

Innie could understand the cold and hungry parts.
Katie had probably spent the missing money on food.
"What about the teapot? Why did you take that?"

"I didn't mean to take it. I thought I was taking only
a small box of food. I'd no idea there was a silver teapot

wrapped up inside. And then I dropped it and bent the handle. I didn't want to give it back broken. I have it hidden, back there, in a barrel of mucky clay." She pointed toward the back of the basement. "Perhaps it can be mended, but I haven't any money."

Innie thought about what she'd heard. Katie seemed to be telling the truth. It would be easy enough to find that teapot now that they knew where to look.

"What will you do with me?" Katie stared at each girl in turn, her green eyes filled with worry. "You won't tell the police, will you? They'll send me back to Ireland just like that." She snapped her fingers.

"I . . . I don't know," Innie said. "But . . ."

"Maybe we can go to the Irish church," Matela began. "That Father we talk to, he might . . ."

Innie put her finger to her lips and shook her head. She didn't want to have to explain all that to Teresa.

"I know what we need to do," Teresa said. Her voice wasn't loud, but it sounded quite decided.

Katie studied Teresa's face. "And what would that be?"

"We'll tell my sister, Carmela. She's just turned into a citizen. She'll know what to do."

"But, Teresa—" Innie began.

"No, Innie. You've been bossing me around my whole life. It's my turn to decide something. I'm going to get Carmela right now, whether you like it or not."

Teresa pointed to the old door, which stood slightly

ajar. "I'll walk out that tunnel all by myself if I have to."
She stood, squared her shoulders, and stepped toward the
door. But just as she reached it, the door swung open.

Carmela stepped into the room. "It's all right, little
sister. I'm already here."

CHAPTER 14
A THURSDAY AFTERNOON GIRL

Carmela! How did you . . ."

"What, Innie? You think I don't have a brain? Teresa's been acting suspicious all day. And tonight, sure, it's nice outside, but not so nice you'd want the window open. But Teresa, she opened it all the way. I knew she was going to sneak out again, so I pretended to sleep."

"You followed us." Teresa's face colored.

"Yes. I followed you. I guessed you were coming to the settlement house." She looked at the little group, then back at Teresa. "Could I meet your friends?"

Teresa nodded. "Sure. Carmela, this is Matela Rosen. She's a Wednesday afternoon girl with us. She's been helping us look for, well, clues."

"And this is Katie," Innie explained. "She's the one leaving the clues."

"So I heard." Carmela nodded. "We're going upstairs. The ladies will have the surprise of their lives."

"The ladies? But, Carmela, they're Yankees," Innie said. "They'll tell the police—"

"Innie, wise up. The ladies spend all their time helping girls like us. They'll know what to do." She turned. "Katie, don't worry. This is a settlement house. A place for immigrant girls to be safe and learn about America. You picked a good tunnel."

There wasn't much anybody could do but follow Carmela up the stairs. Nobody talked, they just climbed—to the first floor, the second, the third, and finally the fourth. Carmela knocked on the door, hard. "Hello! Miss Brown, Miss Guerrier, it's me, Carmela Moretti."

Innie could hear hurrying footsteps and the click of a lock, and then the door flew open.

"Carmela! Whatever is going on?" Miss Guerrier demanded. "How did you get in? What are all these girls doing here? It's the middle of the night." She wrapped her dressing gown tighter around herself and smoothed her braid.

Just behind her, Innie could see Miss Brown hurrying toward the doorway. She was also dressed in nightclothes with her hair down.

Carmela took a quick step forward. "Miss Guerrier, Miss Brown, please. I know it's night and we shouldn't be here. But my sister and my cousin, they found the person who's been taking things. She's just a girl with no place to go. Please, may we come in?"

Miss Brown led Carmela to a sitting room and a comfortable chair. Innie, Teresa, and Matela followed them into the room and crowded together among the fat pillows of a couch.

Miss Guerrier took charge of Katie, settling her in a small chair next to the fireplace. "Begin at the beginning, please," the lady ordered.

Her face looks hard, Innie thought, *like when she accused me. Poor Katie.*

"I'm Katie Mulrooney, from Limerick in Ireland, and then from Chelsea." As she told her story, the ladies' faces softened. They began to look sorry for Katie.

When Katie finished, Miss Brown stood up. "I, for one, could use a bite to eat. Rest yourself for a moment, Katie. Innie, come help."

Innie scrambled to the kitchen and set mugs on a tray. Miss Brown filled them with milk and set out a plate of oatmeal cookies.

Once everyone had been served, Innie settled back on the couch, and Miss Brown turned to Katie. "Now, Miss Mulrooney, perhaps you'll tell us why didn't you stay at one of the churches or schools that's helping people whose homes burned. Why did you hide in the tunnel?"

"I couldn't go to the shelters, Miss. They write down your name and age in those places."

"And why can't you give your name and age?" asked Miss Guerrier.

"I'm young, Miss. Not yet fourteen. Too young to hold a real job. And without one, why the police or the immigration service, they might send me back. And I can't go back. I just can't." Katie hid her face.

"I'm not sure I understand. Did you arrive illegally?" Miss Brown's voice was soft.

Katie sighed. "I'm not sure. We paid a man to help me come here, a Mr. Thomas McKean. He found me work as well but warned me not to say how old I am. I paid a dollar each week to him for the job, but even he's gone now."

Good riddance to him, Innie thought. A dollar a week! That was a day's wages for Carmela.

"You were working as a domestic, I assume?" asked Miss Guerrier.

"Aye. Lots of Irish girls come here to work in fine houses. We save up our wages, you see, to bring over the rest of the family. I'd saved a bit of money, but it all burned in the fire."

Miss Brown nodded her head. "The rest of your family is still in Ireland, then?"

"Aye. Me mum's a widow, Miss, and I've three younger sisters. They're needing the money I was to be making in America. I must have another job, you see, but how can I now, looking like this?" She held up her stained skirt, then let it drop.

Innie looked at Teresa, then at Matela. In Italian families, the men came over first, like Nonna's *bordanti*.

Matela's father had also come ahead to earn money for the family's tickets. It was impossible for Innie to imagine a girl coming to America all alone.

"When will you be fourteen?" Miss Guerrier asked.

"In July. But I can't wait that long to get work. Me family's counting on me. And I . . . I must repay you for what I've taken."

A slight frown creased Miss Guerrier's forehead. "Three months. That's not so long. Do you read well, Katie?"

"Aye. I've got schooling."

That's an odd question, Innie thought. What did reading have to do with being fourteen or working as a maid?

Miss Guerrier continued. "Miss Brown, don't we need another reader in the pottery? Couldn't we use a second voice when we begin reading Shakespeare's plays aloud? We couldn't pay much, but until you're fourteen it would be something . . ."

"You mean you'd hire me to *read*? And after me taking things from your house and all? I'm sorry for that, I am. I'll return your teapot right away. It's hidden in the basement."

"We understand," Miss Brown said gently. "We have a small empty room on the third floor where you could stay. And if you wish to return to domestic work once you're old enough, we will help you find a proper situation." Miss Brown looked at Miss Guerrier, then went on. "That Thomas McKean, he's been taking advantage of you. These things go on, and it is up to us to stop it. We shall inform the authorities about Mr. McKean."

"What a night this has been," Miss Guerrier said. "But I'll be glad to see my teapot again, Katie. Even gladder to see you safe and warm instead of huddling down in that basement."

"If you think the basement's bad, you should see the tunnel," Teresa said. "It smells terrible in there."

"It goes under the burying ground," Innie added. "And there's a sword."

Miss Guerrier sat up straight. "A sword? You found a tunnel, an intruder, and a sword? You've been rather busy, Innie."

"Matela found the sword. It's big, and it looks really old. We can get it for you, Miss Guerrier, but we'll need more candles."

"Well, well," Miss Brown said. "This could be quite a discovery. For years, I've heard rumors of tunnels under the North End. Smugglers' tunnels from before the Revolution. Colonists didn't like paying the taxes on foreign goods, you see, so they smuggled items off the ships to bypass the customs house . . ."

"Smugglers' tunnels? From the old days?" Innie was so excited she could barely get the words out.

Miss Guerrier nodded. "Mrs. Storrow, the lady who owns this house and supports the library clubs, has friends at the museum. I'm sure they'll be fascinated by the secret tunnel and the sword. If the weapon is from colonial days, they might even purchase it for their collection."

Miss Brown smiled. "Indeed. Such a purchase might go a long way toward replacing the money Katie lost in the fire and buying her a new set of clothes. I think that's quite a night's work, myself."

She stood, and everybody else did the same. "Now, Carmela, you'll escort our three Wednesday afternoon girls home safely, I presume."

She turned to Katie. "And you will stay here with us. Beginning Monday, you'll start your reading, and you'll be able to join our library club as well—you'll be a Thursday afternoon girl. Good night, all of you." Miss Brown led Katie toward the kitchen, and Miss Guerrier escorted the others out.

Innie practically ran down all three flights of stairs. She would have slid the whole way on the banister if Miss Guerrier hadn't come along to unlock the door.

Miss Guerrier smiled as she opened the door for them. "My apologies, Innie. Miss Brown and I suspected you, and you were innocent of wrongdoing. We are both truly, truly sorry. Sleep well, and we'll see you on Wednesday afternoon."

The girls stepped out into the warm night, and Innie darted across the street, unable to simply walk.

Carmela and the others followed right on her heels. "There's one thing I still don't understand," Carmela said, taking hold of Innie's arm. "And we're not going home until you explain. Matela, you're Jewish, aren't you?"

"Yes."

"Why did you go to see an Irish priest, then? I heard you say that when I was hiding behind the old door."

Matela looked at Innie.

"It's a long story," Innie began.

"We have all night," Carmela answered.

Innie shook her head. In a family like hers, keeping a secret was harder than finding a room to be quiet in. Maybe that was the price a person paid for belonging to a family. Once again, she explained about the visit to Charlestown.

As she spoke, she noticed Teresa's eyes on her, barely blinking. "Innie, did you really think they'd make you into a Sister, whether you wanted it or not? That would be scary."

"I didn't know any better."

"So that's why you've been such a troublemaker?" Carmela asked. "To stay out of the convent?"

Innie nodded. She didn't trust herself to speak.

"You'll be good now?" Carmela wasn't going to let up, not even a speck.

"A little bit good," Innie said, shrugging as if it didn't really matter. "Nonna would get too suspicious if I was perfect."

"Don't worry, Innie." Carmela laughed and threw an arm around her shoulder. "Nobody expects perfect.

Besides, the house would get boring without your mischief."

"But, Carmela," Innie said, "don't I make you mad?"

"Sure, sometimes. But you stand up to that big-mouth Antonio. Mostly you make me smile," Carmela said. "Everybody needs to smile."

With a running start, Innie jumped onto the stone wall that ran along the sidewalk between the burying ground and the church. Flinging her arms out for balance, she danced along the wall. Behind her, she could hear Matela and Teresa climb onto the wall, giggling. They began stepping along in time.

Carmela shook her head and laughed so loud it filled the night. And then, unbelievably, she too climbed the wall and danced along the smooth stones. "A girl like you, Innocenza Maria Moretti, you even cheer up the graveyard. First you turn me into an American partner. Now you get me out at midnight without any brothers to watch over me. *Grazie,* Innie. *Grazie.*"

A Peek into the Past

PAUL·REVERE·POTTERY
MADE·AT·THE
SATURDAY·EVENING·GIRLS'
BOWL·SHOP

18·HULL·STREET
BOSTON·MASSACHUSETTS

LOOKING BACK: 1908

The Chelsea fire of 1908 left more than 17,000 people homeless.

The Chelsea fire really happened. It began just north of Boston, Massachusetts, on the morning of Sunday, April 12, 1908. Smoke filled the skies all the way to New Hampshire, and tongues of flame could be seen from hilltops and roofs all over Boston. The fire raged into the night, destroying more than 2,800 buildings.

Miss Guerrier, Miss Brown, and the library clubs at 18 Hull Street really existed, too. A Boston woman, Mrs. Helen Storrow, bought the building to create a settlement house for girls from the North End. Most girls—like the fictional Innie, Teresa, and Matela—were daughters of Italian and Jewish immigrants.

Settlement houses were a new idea in the early 1900s. Immigrants were flooding into the United States, settling in poor, crowded city neighborhoods. Settlement houses helped thousands adjust to life in America. Most famous was

An immigrant girl from Italy, and travel documents carried by new arrivals

Chicago's Hull House, started by Jane Addams, but pioneering women in many cities opened settlement houses. They offered English classes for adults, courses for boys in trades like woodworking and printing, and instruction for girls in cooking and sewing.

Jane Addams

Mrs. Storrow's settlement house in Boston was unique, however—it was just for girls! Most settlement houses provided more services for boys, but Mrs. Storrow believed girls were important. And she wanted to teach them more than the skills needed to be housewives or servants. She believed that rigorous learning would give them the best chance to improve their lives.

Mrs. Storrow hired two remarkable women to turn her vision into reality—Edith Guerrier and Edith Brown. Both were educated but of very modest means, so they had great sympathy for girls from poor families.

Miss Guerrier's library clubs succeeded immediately. Girls discussed books and politics, participated in choral singing, learned folk dancing, and practiced needlework. The clubs were named for their meeting times— for example, 12-year-olds met on Wednesdays, so they were known as "Wednesday Afternoon Girls."

Hull Street in 1906. The settlement house is the tallest building on the right. At left is the burying ground fence. Old North Church rises in the background.

Girls in Miss Guerrier's library club practice folk dancing in 1913.

The library clubs were not always popular with parents, however. Many parents thought children should spend their time working, not reading. Some girls, like Innie, really did have to hide their books from strict families.

In 1908, Boston children were required to attend school through age 14. Many immigrant children took full-time jobs as soon as they turned 15, because their families were desperately poor and needed the children's wages to survive. So for older girls, Miss Guerrier and Miss Brown held library clubs in the evenings.

These girls usually worked in crowded sweatshops sewing clothing or in filthy, dangerous factories. To create better jobs for them, Miss Guerrier and Miss Brown established the Paul Revere Pottery. Miss Brown

Girls gather for a library club meeting.

trained young women like Carmela to make and decorate pottery. The girls—known as Saturday Evening Girls—earned up to $10 a week, as much as they could have made in the factories. They enjoyed a clean, well-lit workplace, were served a hot lunch, and listened to classical music, poetry, or Shakespeare while they hand-painted bowls, plates, and vases. Each girl signed her work

on the bottom with her name and "SEG,"
for "Saturday Evening Girl." The pieces
were sold in a shop at the settlement
house and fetched excellent prices.

Outside the settlement house, immigrant life could be harsh. Immigrants often
lived in *tenements* — old, run-down three-story
or four-story apartment buildings packed
tightly along narrow streets. A family of ten

A plate and vase made by Saturday Evening Girls

might share three rooms. To help pay the rent, many families took in lodgers, usually men anxious to save their wages
and bring their families to America. Beds filled every tenement room, even the kitchen. Plumbing was scarce — all
the families in a building shared a single sink in the front
hall and one privy in the basement or under the sidewalk.
Under these conditions, bugs and rodents thrived.

In Boston, many immigrants settled in the North End,
where Innie's story takes place. In 1908, two-thirds of the
North End's 30,000 residents were
Italian Catholics
like the Morettis
who had left Italy
because of political
and economic trou-
bles. The other third
were Jews like Matela's
family, who had left
Russia to escape
religious persecution.

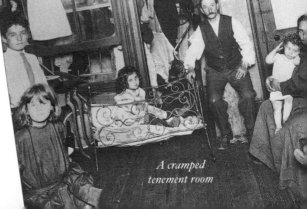

*A cramped
tenement room*

In Russia, Jews were kept away from cities by law, so many Jewish families lived in *shtetls*. These rural villages were frequently terrorized or even burned to the ground by government soldiers who rode in on horseback wielding swords and flaming torches. A family like Matela's had good reason to be cautious around people of different backgrounds.

An Italian immigrant family in 1905

Most immigrants settled in neighborhoods where people from their own country lived. They rarely socialized outside their own ethnic and religious groups. But at the library clubs and the pottery, girls from different backgrounds mingled. As they sang, read, and worked together—Italians and Russians, Catholics and Jews—they forged lifelong friendships. Their children became friends, and today, granddaughters and great-granddaughters still speak with pride about the Saturday Evening Girls.

A Jewish home ransacked by Russian soldiers like the one at left

So the vision shared by Helen Storrow, Edith Guerrier, and Edith Brown proved true. With the inspiration of the library clubs, the girls bettered their lives in America. They mastered English, and many went on to become librarians and teachers at a time when few women held professional jobs.

But the immigrant girls and their families paid a price for their successes. As the girls made their way in America, they lost the language and customs of the old world. Connections between the generations were often strained, as grandparents like Nonna clung to the old ways and grew angry when their granddaughters embraced the new.

Yet in Boston's North End, the immigrants' heritage endures. Wonderful Italian restaurants and grocery stores and Russian-Jewish tailor shops line the streets, recalling a time when the journey from the old world was fresh and recent, and the new world was a puzzle, yet to be solved.

Today, Boston's North End is filled with Italian shops and restaurants.

GLOSSARY OF ITALIAN WORDS

bambina *(bahm-BEE-nah)* — little girl, sweetheart

bella mia *(BEL-lah MEE-ah)* — my dearest

bordanti *(bor-DAHN-tee)* — boarders, lodgers

Buona fortuna! *(BWO-nah for-TOO-nah)* — Good fortune!

cannoli *(kahn-NO-lee)* — a dessert made of a thin pancake
wrapped around a sweet, creamy filling

Capisci? *(kah-PEESH)* — Understand? Get it?

cassata *(kah-SAH-tah)* — cake

grazie *(GRAH-tsyeh)* — thank you

Innocenza *(een-no-CHEN-zah)* — a girl's name

La vita è così. *(lah VEE-tah ay KO-see)* — Life is like that;
so it goes.

Mannaggia l'America! *(mahn-NAH-jah lah-MAY-ree-kah)* —
To heck with America!

Molta felicità! *(MOHL-tah fay-LEE-chee-tah)* — Much
happiness!

Nonna *(NOHN-nah)* — Grandma

Per cent'anni! *(payr chen-TAHN-nee)* — For a hundred years!

sì *(see)* — yes

zia *(ZEE-ah)* — aunt

zio *(ZEE-oh)* — uncle

GLOSSARY OF YIDDISH WORDS

Azoy gayt es. *(ah-ZOY gayt es)* — So it goes; that's life.

bubbe *(BUH-beh)* — grandma

Oy vay is mir! *(oy VAY iz meer)* — an expression of surprise or shock

Matela *(MAHT-uh-luh)* — a nickname for the girl's name Matel

mazik *(MAH-zik)* — a spirit that causes mischief for human beings

Shabbos *(SHAH-bus)* — the Jewish Sabbath, a day of rest and prayer. It begins at sundown on Friday and ends after sundown on Saturday.

shul *(shul, rhymes with "pull")* — a Jewish house of prayer, a synagogue

AUTHOR'S NOTE

I could not have written this book without several special people. Historian Kate Clifford Larsen has written extensively about the Saturday Evening Girls. She was generous in sharing her work and research sources so that I could learn about the places and times of the story.

Barbara Maysles Kramer, whose mother Ethyl (Epstein) Maysles was a Saturday Evening Girl, welcomed me into her home. She shared stories and photographs from her mother's girlhood and showed me her wonderful collection of pottery made at 18 Hull Street.

Good friends Debbie Roth and Leah Schollar, who is a teacher of Judaic Studies, recalled the old people in their Russian-Jewish families. Elizabeth McCarthy and Donna Zaffy told me of their Italian immigrant grandmothers.

These family stories helped me fill in the details of ordinary life that make a book feel real and interesting. Family stories also remind me that although great events often change the lives of large numbers of people, history also happens one family at a time.